Christopher Kenw

is a full-time writer

has appeared in *A Bo*

Best Fantasy and Horro

many others. In the

Barrington Books, pu

of miserablist fiction. *Will You Hold Me?* is the

first collection of his short stories.

Will You Hold Me?

Christopher Kenworthy

THE DO-NOT PRESS

First Published in Great Britain in 1996 by
The Do-Not Press
PO Box 4215
London SE23 2QD

Collection and stories © 1996 by Christopher Kenworthy
'Because of Dust' was first published in 'The Third Alternative' (Issue 6, 1995), and 'The Year's Best Fantasy and Horror' (1996); 'The Closing Hand' in 'Kimota' (Issue 3, 1996); 'Them Belgiums' in 'A Book of Two Halves' (Gollancz, 1996); and 'Despite The Cold' in 'Time Out Net Books' (Issue 6, 1996)
All other stories are original to this collection.

ISBN 1 899344 11 X

British Library Cataloguing in Publication Data. A catalogue record for this book is available from the British Library.

Printed and bound in Great Britain by The Guernsey Press Co Ltd.

Contents

Thanks…

to all those who helped with my writing, one way or another, especially David Clarke, Andy Cox, Ellen Datlow, Jim Driver, Colin Greenland, Stuart Kenworthy, Mum and Dad, Joel Lane, Mark Morris, Tim Nickels, Shareena Rahim, Nicholas Royle, Geoff Ryman, and Conrad Williams.

Because of Dust

When I think about Rachel I remember being locked out of my car with her on the Derwent Water car park. It was warmer than you'd think possible for October, the sunset dissipating while we waited for the AA recovery van to arrive. I kept apologising, but she said it didn't matter. I'd only known her for one full day, but she wrapped her arms around me, making me acutely aware of her thin breasts pressing against my chest. As the air grew colder, the contact warmed our skin.

I'd met her a week previously at the Corner House cinema in Manchester. They were launching a new fiction magazine the same night, upstairs, so the theatre itself was virtually empty. The film was Spanish, so I needed the subtitles. Reading them isn't normally a problem for me, but they were lower than usual on the screen, and every time I read a line my attention fixed on the back of somebody's head. She had blonde hair, which was an obvious distraction. There was no movement from her until the credits ran, and then she wiped one hand around the back of her head, lifting her hair so that I caught a glimpse of neck.

I don't normally go into the bar on my own, but when I saw her venture in alone, I followed. She sat at a large table, which gave me an excuse to share it with her, because the smaller ones were crowding up.

'Did you enjoy that?' she asked.

I looked up from the programme sheet, which I was pretending to read.

'Oh yes. The bit where the boy walked up behind the woman hitcher, so slowly. Wonderful.'

She nodded, then smiled. I wanted to ask her if she came here often, quite simply because I was curious to know why I'd never seen her before, but it was such a cliché that I didn't speak.

I read my programme again, drinking frequently, trying to think of something less predictable to ask, but a few minutes later she rescued me by saying, 'I've got to catch my train now,' as she sidled out from behind the table.

Without thinking or hesitating I asked if she'd like to go out some time. I knew my expression was going to change from one of blank abandon to a pathetic sort of nervous query, but she said yes quickly, which was a relief.

It turned out that we were both free the following Sunday. I'd been planning to go to the Lakes, not for any serious walking, just a wander, and she said she'd love to go. Hadn't been up there since she was seven.

'Where do you live?' I asked.

'Hebden Bridge. It's in the middle of nowhere, but there are plenty of trains. I can meet you at your local station, early on.'

We swapped phone numbers and she left. I drank slowly in case she missed her train and came back, but soon the bar lights were switched off, making me realise the time. It started to rain, a thin summery type of rain, not at all cold, and I smiled all the way back to my car.

*

On the way back from the Lakes we stopped at the Tebay service station, and over two treacly coffees, Rachel gave me a sugar cube; in fact it was a packet of two cubes, held together in a rectangle of white wrapping with a red T logo.

'It's a present,' she said.

'I'll treasure it.'

I'm sure she knew the intimacy of her gesture, because she looked into my eyes for a long time, but I don't know if she realised how tightly I'd hold on to her gift.

There is a shelf in my house where I store the few important objects that have been given to me. They are all soaked with memories, and when I put them in my hands I relive the moments when people offered slithers of themselves.

On the left is Mark's feather, held down with a blob of Blu-tac. We were staying in London at the time, during a relentless summer. The streets were coated with fine sand, as though the dry air had sapped so much water from the town it was starting to crumble. He picked a feather up as we headed for the Seven Sisters tube. It was mostly black, with a smear of orange and green along one edge. We debated whether it was real or dyed. Despite a lack of free-flying tropical birds in the city, we decided it was genuine, and he gave it to me.

'Look after that,' he said.

When I hold the feather now I can smell the sweaty diesel scent of the tube, and I remember sitting next to Mark, looking at each other in reflection on the other side of the carriage as we talked. We laughed so much that we missed our stop and had to walk from Tottenham Court Road to Foley Street, making us late for the party.

Next to the feather are stones that Nick and Decko gave to me. I'd never been on a beach with so many different types of stone. For half an hour we picked out flat rocks and skimmed them on the lulling green waves which shattered around us, making us run back to preserve our feet. When the air softened with rain we exchanged stones. Nick gave me a dull pebble the colour of brick. Decko's stone looked like melted porcelain, with a vein of rouge.

If I hold those stones now, one in each hand, I can remember details I wasn't even aware of at the time; the seagulls key-shifting song, the stink of marshland behind us, and the murmur of an ice cream van's engine, parked close by, its beige and red paint seeming to grow brighter as the ashen clouds turned black.

Rachel's sugar cube is on the right of the shelf, and when I touch it, my memories are bewildered; my eyes grow wet before I know what to think.

I only knew Rachel for one full day, so it's difficult to understand why she had such an effect on me. Within an hour of her climbing into the car, within ten minutes even, we relaxed. Instead of talking about who we were and what we did, we talked about what we'd seen on the news last night, the things we could see out of the windows. We talked about small details. Normally it takes weeks for a relationship to settle into this sort of familiarity, but by the time we passed Forton Services, with its Magic Roundabout tower, I felt certain we weren't going to stumble.

With anybody else I would have felt a need to do specific things, to plan a series of events to prevent awkward silences. With some people in the past I'd even memorised lists of subjects to talk about, so that we wouldn't struggle. It's a shabby technique. How many times have I asked people what records they like, only to be worryingly disappointed? If somebody tells you that they like Barry Manilow on a first date, it's going to make you back off before you have any idea about your feelings for them. When you love somebody, such things are endearing.

I couldn't face another conversation asking what films somebody liked, whether they played a musical instrument, where they went to university, how they got on with their parents. I never asked Rachel any of these questions, and she didn't ask me. At the end of the day I knew very few facts about her, but I saw the way she ran her hands through the grass as we sat by Derwent Water, and knew more than if she had given me a history of preferences.

We drove up to Keswick along the astounding curves of the A66, where the west coast mountains are jagged silhouettes with a frosting of mist over them.

'I can't believe this weather,' I said.

It was warm enough to wear T-shirts, and there were no clouds until late afternoon, though something about it being autumn made the air feel clean. We found a quiet place, south of Friar's Crag. The ground was dry and we sat there for hours, leaning against a tree, picking at the grass, fiddling with stones, listening to brittle leaves peeling from the trees and landing on the water. The lake itself was still, mercifully free of boats. The sun went behind Cat Bells cooling the valley with shadow.

Walking back to the car the air became so still that I stopped to watch the lake. Its surface was without ripples, one sheet of unmoving white.

A grassed area led down to the water. Rachel followed me and stood to the side as I knelt close to the edge, putting my hands through the surface. Its fragile skin gave way and I put my arms in, almost to the elbow. Rings of dark circled outwards from me.

I drew my hands out when they were too cold, and droplets fell away. A few strips of transparent jelly remained on my skin like blisters of glass. I realised they were leeches and wiped them off on the turf.

My arms were dry by the time we reached the car, but after standing outside for twenty minutes waiting for the AA, we were both frozen, apart from the places where our bodies pressed.

It was fully dark as we drove down the M6, and Rachel insisted that I drop her at Preston railway station. I kept offering to run her all the way.

'You'll be up all night,' she said. 'Trust me, there's a late train. I'll be okay. My house is one bus ride from the station, so I'll be quite safe.'

She countered all my planned arguments, so I could only say, 'But I'd like to run you back.'

'I don't like the thought of you driving home so late,' she said, and her concern made me want to grin.

At the station she wouldn't even let me see her on to the platform.

'I'll wait a few minutes, in case you've missed it,' I said.

'I'll be fine.'

She was standing outside the car, leaning in to talk, which made it impossible for us to kiss. I smiled as she slammed the door and gave a wave. I looked round to see her one last time, but she'd already gone through.

*

I was absolutely certain that Rachel said she'd phone me, but when a week had passed I almost gave up on her.

Each night I promised to do something useful, even to go out, but I stayed in with the TV on, dying for the phone to ring. People did ring, proving that the line was working, but Rachel never called.

I was determined to wait for her, not out of stubbornness, but because I didn't want to look pushy.

It had happened to me once before, with Anna. I'd known Anna for about two years, vaguely, because she worked in my local newsagent's. I always felt there was something movingly significant about the fact that my first words to her had been, 'Guardian, please.' I was sure this meant we were fated to have a relationship. She agreed to go out with me for a drink when I finally asked, but we found each other unbearably dull. We both toyed with beer-mats in The Anchor while she told me that she played the organ, and that she liked Barry Manilow. At first I made polite comments about this, to fill the gaps in the conversation, but once I'd had a couple of drinks I asked her what the appeal was, made references to his nose. She said I was being a bit predictable.

For some reason we both tried to keep the momentum going, and went back to my place. Our conversation was even more nervous, and when I finally got round to kissing her, my arm over her back felt uncomfortable. It was the same sense of unease I feel when holding other people's children; a total lack of familiarity. Her lips, although soft, were narrow and didn't move much.

I rang Decko the next day and told him that she kissed like a frog. This was rude, but it indicated to me that I shouldn't let it go any further. Strangely, after I got off the phone to him I went to the bathroom and found a frog perched on the side of the toilet bowl. This unnerved me.

A week after having declared that she kissed like a frog, and determining not to see her again, I was desperate for her to ring. I finally decided that I would call, just in case she had lost my number, but before I had worked out how to word it my brother rang me up. He'd seen Anna in town with another man.

'It could be her brother,' he said, 'but they were holding hands.'

Since then I've bought my newspapers elsewhere.

I decided that despite the risk of repeating history, I would call Rachel, just to see if she still had my number. After all, she could be sitting there hoping I'd get in touch, wondering what she did with that slip of paper. I might even give in and say that I couldn't wait for her to ring.

I barely knew her, but was quite obsessed. With Anna I'd been keen to see her again, even though we didn't get on, because of her sudden unavailability, her refusal to reconnect. With Rachel, my enthusiasm was for the way she made me feel. I liked the simplicity of this.

The voice that answered had a slight accent, similar to Rachel's, but sounded older.

'Is Rachel there please?'

There was a sound of swallowing.

'Hello?' I tried, but only heard the same sound, and then the phone was put down.

I tried the number again, quite annoyed, but at the same time worried. It rang six times before it was picked up, and I could hear sobbing at the other end.

'Are you a friend?' the voice said, her breath catching.

'Yes.'

'I'm so sorry,' she said. 'Rachel died last Monday. She was buried today.'

I felt that I ought to keep talking, to be polite, but a silence followed where I could hear our breathing mingle in the phone.

More than anything I was astounded that it happened on Monday, the day after we parted. I was frightened by the thought that I'd been picturing her alive, doing things, when she'd been in a mortuary.

'What did she die of?' I asked.

'Her headaches, finally,' the voice said, breaking up. I caught the word 'haemorrhage' which was enough to clarify her meaning.

'I'm her mother,' she said, and I couldn't help but notice that she was using the wrong tense.

When I managed to get off the phone I was aware that my whole body was hot with sweat, and that my stomach had glued with something heavy. I'd never known anybody die, not even my parents. Having known Rachel such a short time didn't make it seem any better. I felt more cheated than if I'd been treated to a few years with her.

I experienced curiously selfish and sexual thoughts, such as annoyance at the fact that I would never know what her nipples looked like. I would never know how she kissed or what she smelt like after sex. I wanted to be able to put my hands on her belly while she breathed in sleep. I'd never even see her washing her hair.

It was difficult to picture her without imaging her being in the coffin. It would take a while for her body to rot fully, but I knew the initial sourness would have set in. They say that the softer parts give way first. The eyes moisten and slush, while the mouth, anus and vagina widen into mouldy clefts. Already, decay would have made her hideous.

In my bedroom I clutched the sugar cube with my eyes closed, and smelt water, petrol, and something like warm wood, which I remembered was her hair.

*

Heading east on the train, the countryside lost its colour. Autumn leafed trees gave way to barren trunks. There was old snow, dirtied and patchy, chimneys grizzling smoke into the sunless layering of cloud.

Hebden Bridge confused me because there weren't enough signs to find my way around. The roads surrounding the canal were all being worked on, so that amongst the pollution stained buildings, were endless bright rags of safety ribbons and tangles of orange plastic fencing. The JCBs and earth movers were abandoned, their joints looking frozen.

The bus ride up to Heptonstall was unnerving, because the back wheels skidded over the cobbles, and we drove up roads that I felt were too steep even to walk on. The bus driver indicated the stop I had asked for.

'There you are love,' he said. I'd only been to Yorkshire once, and it took me a while to get used to men calling other men 'love', but when he said it, I appreciated the kindness in his voice.

I'd talked to Rachel's mother again on the phone, and she was horrified that I had missed the funeral.

'I tried to call her friends,' she said, her jerky breath crackling down the line, 'but there weren't many I could trace. She didn't keep an address book. She memorised numbers and names.'

'Were there many people at the funeral?'

'No. Not many.'

She insisted that I go over and stop with her. I agreed, saying that I wanted to see the grave.

She said: 'There's more for you to see than that.'

The house was set back from the road, down a stone path. Where there had once been a lawn, the ground was completely dug over, ploughed ridges cradling granular snow.

Rachel's mother opened the door and a hot rush of cooking wafted out. She was as tall as me but quite wide. She squinted permanently, and the wrinkles worsened when she tried to smile.

'I'm so glad you came.'

I felt disoriented, again reminding myself how brief my relationship with Rachel had been, but knowing that I wanted more. I couldn't bear to let it end at that. I wanted to recover something of her.

By the time Mrs Clarke had fed me scones and cake, along with several cups of dandelion tea, I knew it was too late to venture out to the grave. It was only just past six o'clock, but it had been dark since three.

She told me all sorts of stories about Rachel and her father. I smiled, nodded, added words of encouragement, but really I wanted to get some sleep.

'How did you know her?' she finally asked.

'It's difficult to say. Did she ever mention me?'

'Not by name.'

I realised how ridiculous this was, because she wouldn't have had time to tell her mother anything about me.

'We both shared an interest in films,' I said, worried that the formality of the phrase would reveal its lack of sincerity.

The woman nodded slowly.

'Did you love her?' she asked.

The question shocked me less than I would have thought. That she asked it wasn't much of a surprise, but the fact that I had to think before I could answer startled me.

'I don't really know,' I said, my throat becoming hard. 'I didn't really have time.'

I took the plates into the kitchen and washed them. Trying to look out of the window into blackness I found it difficult to see anything. There were cobwebs and flies stuck to the other side of the glass, and a couple of moths flickered against the surface. I saw myself in the reflection then, noticing that my posture had lowered and my face was thin.

Leaning round the door to the front room, I said, 'I think I'd better get some sleep, before tomorrow.'

'I'll put you in the spare room,' she said. 'It's next to Rachel's. I haven't been in there since she died. It's still a mess. I can't face cleaning it up.'

'I'll clear up in there if you like.'

Her face sagged first, and even as she smiled at my request, her eyes were shiny with tears.

'You're welcome to look through her things,' she said.

It was a peculiar thing to say, so I kept quiet for a few moments, until she led me to the spare room. I didn't expect to sleep at all because the room was freezing, but as soon as I had curled up under the itchy blankets, I fell into it dreamless.

*

I woke at half past six and the curtains were full of amber

light. Outside there was a black and white valley, a new covering of snow over the coal coloured ground, making the trees look sharp. A pool of mist had settled in the valley and the rising sun sent warmth through it. Sun rises have more clarity than sunsets, more like a concentrated shine instead of a wash. The sun turned red as it rose, then became a colourless circle as I watched the sky becoming blue, dampening with cloud.

My skin felt warm, but the room was still cold enough for my breath to form clouds.

I dressed without washing, because I was trying to be quiet, then went to Rachel's room. It was smaller than the one I'd slept in, but much warmer. There was a wardrobe, a cupboard with mirrors, and a bed. There were no posters on the walls. I examined the bottles of deodorant, perfume and moisturiser by the mirror, disappointed that this was so familiar and ordinary a bedroom.

I chose a jar of Vitamin E Facial Cream and unscrewed the cap. Inside, the sticky stuff was swirled where her fingers had been. It smelt sweet, and as I looked closer I could see tiny lines left by the passing of her fingerprint.

I wanted to look at her clothes, to imagine her wearing them. When I opened the top drawer I found piles of folded white underwear. The bras were on one side, panties on the other. I lifted a pair out, their softness giving me an erection which made me frown with guilt. As I put the knickers back I noticed a slight yellowing along the gusset and closed the drawer quickly.

Until then I hadn't noticed anything wrong with the bed, and it took a few moments of staring to work out what was bothering me. The bed hadn't been made since Rachel was lifted from it, and there was an impression of her in the duvet. On the pillow there was a wide stain, which I thought must be blood.

The material was cold when I touched it, in contrast to the heat of the room, and I knew then that the room couldn't give me what I needed, so went downstairs.

From the front room I could see the church and the edge of the graveyard, about a minute's walk away. I would need hot water, so I went back into the kitchen. It was clear now why I hadn't been able to see anything out there at night; the kitchen window looked into an old conservatory. Each pane was mottled with something that looked like birdlime. The window-sills were lined with potted plants, all long dead, the soil dried so deeply that you could see their white roots, like grubs. Between the plants were hundreds of dead flies, scattered like raisins. I noticed the sound of those that were still alive, which until then I had presumed to be the hiss of the fridge. Some were spinning on their backs, legs jiggling.

Flies and moths circled wildly, a concentration of them in the far left-hand corner, crawling over the wood. I couldn't work out what they could be eating in there, or why there were so many.

The prospect of going in there to clear the place out was obviously too much for Mrs. Clarke. It must have been too much for Rachel as well, because they seemed to have been gathering for months. I thought that I would make an attempt to sweep the worst of them away, before going home. Depending on what happened at the grave.

I found a plastic bucket in a cupboard, took the mop out of it, then filled it with hot water. I squirted some Ecover into it and left the house without spilling any. The snow was difficult to walk on, especially as it had settled on ice, but as this meant I had more chance of being alone, I didn't mind. The bucket steamed like a nitrogen experiment on Tomorrow's World. I remember they used to put soft things, like fruit, into the liquid, and then shattered them with a hammer, for effect.

The church building wasn't impressive, but the old grave-yard was unique. Where grass would usually be, the ground was plated with fallen headstones, more piled on top of them, leaning around and against each other. They reminded me of Stonehenge, and I remembered something Rachel told me. She said that because worms create holes in the ground, depositing dust on the surface, they are slowly burying everything we have built. Stonehenge, she told me, was sinking at the rate of six inches per century.

'Just because of dust?' I asked.

'Yes. They bring minerals up from below, for the plants, and all the stones go deeper. That's why old lawns and meadows are always free of stones, if you dig into them.'

Round the back of the church I found the new field, only half scarred with graves. The last one was Rachel's, the soil mound having sagged into itself. I'd imagined more flowers, but there were only two roses, one bright yellow, the other a damaged brown. Both were rotten with frost, welded to the soil with ice. I chiselled some of the ice away with my fingertips, and pulled the brown one free. The outer crusting fell away, revealing petals as red as flesh.

There was nobody around, so I lifted the bucket and poured its contents along the length of the soil. I didn't know whether it would be better to concentrate on one area, or spread it over her whole length. In the end I put more water in the place where I thought her head would be. The bucket had been heavy and difficult to carry, but once empty I was concerned that there wasn't nearly enough liquid to achieve the desired effect.

I needn't have worried, because the first worm heads appeared within moments. Earthworms don't really have heads, but because there is a fold of nerves in the end which burrows, it's fair enough to think of it as a head. They don't have eyes either, which is probably why we think of them as being without true life or personality. When I was a teenager I charmed worms from the soil, then pulled them apart. Sometimes I'd cut them into several pieces, to see which squirmed the most. Invariably the gristle coloured part, which controlled circulation, was the piece which moved the least. The other segments coiled and wriggled until they dried out.

Although they are pink, it's difficult to think of worms as containing blood. Their blood is similar to ours; it even shares our haemoglobin. As they nosed on to the surface, I hoped these worms would share much more.

I guessed they had already cast a layer of Rachel's dust over the surface, in the days before I arrived. Although she wouldn't have rotted much, part of her would probably have melted through the base of the coffin, so that some of her essence was available to the soil. By bringing the worms out from there, I could gain access to her, put the moment of her into my hand.

The worms were slippery but covered with crumbs of dirt. They reminded me of something intestinal, a mass of peristalsis. Roiling on the mud they looked drugged. I gathered them up, watching their bodies fatten and shrink as they oozed around my fingers.

I remembered the sound of Rachel's voice and her small laugh, the smell of her T-shirt, perfumed by skin as we hugged in the darkening trees. I remembered the orange flashing lights of the AA van on her smiling face, and the tightening of her hug before she let go. She held my hand, for a second. I saw her face clearly, and knew that her eyes weren't watching me; they were looking into mine.

The sky was clear, blue as twilight, and despite the snow and ice I was aware of how grassy this field was. The worms shrank, turning white. In my hands they felt sharp nosed, like maggots. As the sun warmed on to my back the church bell began to chime.

*

I put the bucket away before Rachel's mother came through. We stood in the kitchen while she slotted bread into the toaster. I told her that I'd already been to the grave, and that I would be going soon.

'But you'll stay for breakfast.'

'Yes, and then I'll go.'

She lowered the bread with a metallic springing sound, and I could swear I heard the fibres of it drying out.

In the conservatory moths and flies rattled against the glass, and I tried to look away from them.

Sunlight came into the kitchen, showing up dust in the air. Somebody once told me that ninety percent of dust is skin. I often wonder what the other ten percent is. The way those particles sparkled, I thought they could have been gold.

The Mathematics
of the Night

Waking up, I noticed several things one after the other, which were slightly abnormal. The window at the end of our room was open, curtains parted by cool air. It was a clear day, the buildings on the other side of the Rue de Bievre white with morning light. I was holding hands with somebody, my right hand draped over my back, comfortably, and her fingers held in mine. It was an unusual caress, something I never did. There was no other contact, no sound of breathing or weight of her behind me. When I squeezed, her fingers returned the pressure. It was only when I heard Claire scraping a chair in the kitchen, that I knew she couldn't be in bed with me. I turned to my right, sitting up at the same time, but found I was alone, my hand clutching at itself. I was tempted to feel the sheets for warmth, but instead examined my palm, sniffing at it, trying to detect whose sweat was glittering there. I could only smell my own skin.

I didn't want Claire to see me, because the moment upset me, and I needed to think about it. I wanted to hold hands again, to bring her across the bed, so we were touching all over. If Claire came in and talked about something trivial, or started fighting and tickling, I'd get mad, and the day would be ruined.

The worst thing was that it didn't feel like a dream. I was certain I knew the person who'd been with me, but couldn't remember who she was. I closed my eyes, trying to picture her face, but all I could bring back was the shape of her hand, fitting into mine, holding on.

Claire walked in from the kitchen, still chewing something large, wiping the corners of her mouth as she passed the bed. She was wearing a towelling bathrobe like a dressing gown, and her hair was wet, which meant she must have been up for a while. She turned her back to me, and looked down into the street. Then she turned, smiled and pushed her hair back as she sat by my feet.

'Morning,' she said, in English, and that made me remember. The person I'd been with was French. That was unlikely, though, because my time in Paris had all been spent with Claire. I was never on my own, never met other people.

'Morning,' she snapped. 'Bastard.'

I knew I was in the wrong for ignoring her, but her impatience made me angry, so I held a hand up and said, 'I'm trying to remember something.'

'Piss off then.'

If it hadn't been for the hand I'd held, this would have passed like any other morning row, but the friendliness of that touch made me lonely. I didn't want Claire to come near me, because contact would push the memory even further back. It wasn't fair, waking up with such a feeling, only to have it abandon me. My eyes filmed with tears. It surprised me, and I could tell that I was about to cry, so rushed out of bed naked and went straight to the bathroom.

'Look at that hard-on,' Claire yelled after me. 'Naughty dreams Malcolm?' At first I thought she was trying to make me laugh, so I said, 'I just need a piss,' hoping she hadn't seen the look on my face.

'I bet,' she said, quietly enough to be rude.

'Yes,' I shouted through, doing my best to urinate as loudly as possible, stepping from foot to foot on the freezing tiles, wiping at my face, taking big cold breaths to calm down.

There was quiet for a while, but I couldn't get my mind straight, because I knew Claire wouldn't leave it at that. When she spoke, her voice was resigned, like a sigh. 'Come here,' she called through, and I couldn't tell whether it meant the argument was over, or that we were in for a big one. After a pause, I went back in and hunted for clothes.

'I don't think you want to be here,' she said, lifting her head, chin pointing up, arms folded. This looked a bit ridiculous on her, because her posture was so bad, the top half of her body – skinny though it was – sagging towards her hips. I straightened my own back, because looking at her made me uncomfortable.

I hate arguing when I'm not fully dressed. Perhaps it's

because you can't threaten to walk out when you've only got boxer shorts on. While she watched, waiting for my reaction, I dressed as quickly as possible.

'What do you mean?' I asked pulling on socks, glancing outside. At least the weather was fine. If she kicked me out, I'd be able to wander around for a while, without spending much money. 'Do you want me here?'

'I asked you.' Claire's face was red, not just in the cheeks, but all over, as though she was in a sauna.

I sometimes think of arguments as flow charts, a set of predetermined responses. Given the first two lines of any argument, you can work your way through the link of clichés to the end. One way out for me would be to say sorry, mention a headache, tell her I'd been put in a bad mood by nightmares, say it was my fault. She'd accept, we'd hold each other, it would be put aside.

'Oh this is ridiculous,' I said half-heartedly, lying down to pull my jeans on. 'Of course I don't want to leave.'

Having been awake less than five minutes, it was peculiar to find that we were talking about breaking up. If I left Claire, I'd probably have to leave Paris. That was inevitable in a month anyway. I had money, but it was running out, and before long I'd have to get back to London. There was always more work in winter, and I couldn't keep relying on Claire.

'But it's not as though I'm living with you, is it?' I added. 'I'm only visiting.'

'Visiting?' She lowered her head, eyebrows raised, and held that expression.

I knew this could quickly escalate into blame-swapping, and an argument over who paid how much for what, so I stalled it quickly.

'That's not what I mean. It's not the flat that matters. It's you and me.'

We looked at each other then, me feeling sheepish for having told the truth, Claire surprised. Then she looked sad, and lowered her face into her hands.

'I thought things were going well,' she said.

'They are. They are.'

She smiled with her mouth closed, and went back into the kitchen.

*

Walking down Rue Jussieu, at the back of the glassy Universités building, I rubbed my fingers together, trying to recall a time in my life when I'd been comfortable holding hands. Nothing came to mind. It seemed like a clumsy contact that generally leads to sweating, wiping, awkward moments when passing lampposts. Holding hands in bed was different. It wasn't being done for show or warmth, but because the person I was with wanted to touch me. It was friendly, but could only have been made by somebody willing to be sexual.

It was disappointing to find Rue Cuvier almost empty, because I anticipated hoards of students. Perhaps everybody else was using Jardin des Plantes as their route. Half the fun of walking around Paris is making eye contact with strangers. I kidded myself that I was a people watcher, interested in human interaction, or something, but I really wanted to look for pretty faces. My eye sight is less than perfect – left uncorrected to avoid headaches – which gives me a tendency to stare at people until they are close up. There was nobody to see, and I was running out of places to walk. If it wasn't for the heat of blisters, my feet would be frozen.

Although I'd managed to get through the afternoon quite easily in the Pantheon library, I was bored now, wondering what to do with myself. Claire hadn't kicked me out, but I didn't want to be home before she got back from work. I wanted to make her wait around for me, getting hungry while I was somewhere else. She'd have no idea how I could stay out so long, what I could be doing. She'd wait for me, so that I could cook. She wouldn't be able to pay attention to the TV, her mind wandering too much to translate, so she would sit in the armchair, watching the door, occasionally peering out of the window for me.

I made my breathing shallow as I turned on to the main road, to avoid the icy petrol fumes getting too deep. There were more people around, and I soon made eye contact with a woman who was strolling with her boyfriend. He was leaning around, trying to tell her a story, so excited he was probably spitting on her. The more he leaned the more she looked away, until her face was facing mine. She pretended to listen to his story, but I could tell the smile was directed at me. I was the first to look away, and only after she'd passed could I smell her perfume, something so expensive I had no way of recognising it.

When she was gone I felt foolish for being so excited. The thrill only came from being unfaithful on the inside, not from attraction. It was gutless, like sticking your fingers up behind somebody's back to make yourself feel better. Which was pointless, because it wouldn't affect Claire unless I told her; it would only affect me, make me a little more distant from her.

I felt stupid for avoiding her. She wasn't really to blame, even if she did annoy me at times. I realised it wasn't anger at her, or fear of arguing, that was keeping me away from the flat. It was that I wanted to be on my own. Having being touched the way I was that morning, it would feel wrong to go back to Claire.

It was getting towards four o'clock, the sky becoming bluer, as though I was looking at it through sunglasses. The buildings were tinged with an orange nap, even though the sun was out of sight. My mouth was sticky, which meant I needed to eat. The cafés off Quai Saint Bernard looked too expensive and formal for a snack, so it was a relief to see a chestnut seller. He was huddled in shadow by the walls that ran above the Seine, in an area so dark it was difficult to make him out. His movement was slow, cold looking. When the wind caught the charcoal in his brazier, grey ash flaked off, and it shone like Christmas lights. His face and hands didn't look dirty so much as thick skinned, fingers pushing the chestnuts over the grate, turning them until they split. I asked for a bag full, and he shuffled them up and handed them over without looking at me.

Feeling pleased with my purchase, I went down the steps at Pont De Sully, to the level of the river, where it was quieter. I managed to peel the wooden skin from the chestnuts while walking, the hard edges stabbing under my nails. They were so well cooked that the yellow flesh was creamy, almost like a mild cheese, and it dissolved completely. There were about ten chestnuts in all, and I ate them before they had cooled, burning my finger-ends.

When I had swallowed the last, I crumpled the bag up in my coat pocket, and headed toward the city centre. I don't remember stopping, but after I passed under the next bridge I found myself standing close to the edge of the water, staring.

There was a stillness. The light settling around me. I stood for a long time with no movement. Where there had been a breeze flickering leaves in the bank-side trees, there was calm. Nobody else was around, and I looked at the river, the walls on the opposite side, each window in the buildings, the gardens around Notre Dame trailing ivy into the Seine. Instead of glancing around, my head was still, gaze fixed, but my perception widened so that I could see more. It was bright, everything appearing to be slightly haloed, but I didn't squint. I became aware of my body. The pain of chestnut pericarp under my fingernails. Charcoal flavour in my mouth, from the scorched kernels. A smell of wet coal from the barges which passed earlier. Dryness on my cheeks, skin tanned by cold. Blood in my knees warming the joints, toes uncurling, and my heart, slowing, thumping in response to the deeper opening of my lungs.

I blinked for the first time in minutes, and my eyes watered. As I walked on, wiping my face, I almost forgot what had happened. It was the same as waking from a strange dream. Once remembered, it is unforgettable, but almost, almost, you let it go in your rush to wake up. Heading for the steps up to Pont De Archeveche, I heard traffic again, saw people rushing on the pavements above, and headed that way.

*

Exhausted from swilling three espressos, I tried to walk the caffeine off, the cold addling my brain, bringing on a pleasant dizziness. It was inevitable that I would have to eat, and even though the flat was only a minute away, I wanted to stay out. Le Grenier was my favourite restaurant, but too expensive for regular meals. It would be a treat to order on my own, sit without talking, drink as much as I wanted. Facing Claire after that wouldn't seem so bad.

I hadn't been to Le Grenier for weeks, apart from lunches, but the waitress recognised me, asked if I was alone, and then took me upstairs to my favourite table. The spiral staircase must have broken European safety laws, being so steep it was more like a twisted ladder. There was only one long table, and I was crammed into a corner at the end; I had to slide through a gap and lower myself into place. The waitress lit my candle and I sat back with the menu, the room to myself.

The lampshade over my table was scorched, where its material rested against the bulb. The only sound was small music from speakers I could never locate. The walls were mirrored, probably a throwback to its eighties refurbishment, but it managed to maintain rustic overtones by trailing strings of dried corn-on-the-cob across the ceiling.

Before I'd even ordered, my peace was disturbed. Downstairs, people were laughing and chattering, the sort of communal giggle and banter that suggests an office party. When I heard their first thumping steps on the metal stairs, I knew they were about to fill the room and spoil my meal.

It was worse than I'd feared, because there were thirteen of them, enough to fill every chair. All were younger than thirty, mostly wearing shirts and jeans under camel coats. They didn't look to be celebrating but it seemed a large crowd, if they were just friends going out for a meal. The shuffling off of coats, and moving into seats happened quickly, but rather than saying bonjour or apologising for getting in the way, they sat around me as though I was part of the group, without acknowledgement. I ended up with a man sitting across from me, a woman crushed up to my side, so that I effectively joined them. When I looked up, the man nodded and winked, which was so unusual a gesture, I wondered if he had a twitch. His face was remarkably well shaven, no shadow or scabbing, his skin fleshy, teeth wet. To avoid looking him, I concentrated on the menu, tried not to listen to their conversation.

I decided that if the waitress served them first, and forgot about me, I would get mad. To my relief she came to me, wetting the nib of her pen with her tongue. It was obvious that I was English when I spoke, I suppose, because the crowd quietened for a while as I ordered seaweed and tofu, asking for extra soy sauce. By the time I asked for seitan and potatoes, they were watching me, muttering amongst themselves, so that I ordered a beer quickly and left it at that. The murmuring grew louder to my relief, but when I looked up half of them were smiling at me. Foreigners aren't exactly rare in Paris, so I can only assume they were pleased to see me making an effort with the language.

The waitress carried on writing, before turning to the rest of the crowd. Instead of sending my order down first, she was lumping me in with them. Once the man opposite had ordered, he looked across at me and said something so rapidly, I thought he was speaking Polish.

I held my hands out, trying so hard to comprehend him, I didn't even speak. He grinned and shook his head, then nodded, so that I hadn't a clue what he was on about. He seemed to be under the impression that I had understood him, and continued to watch me, his lips pressing into a pout, tongue occasionally pointing through. The orders were almost in now, and I was longing for my beer, something to stare at and occupy my hands with.

'Herb,' he said to me, holding out his hand, which I shook. His grip was over-firm, but hollow, as though he didn't really like touching me.

'Malcolm,' I said, sitting up in my chair, straightening my knife and fork.

'Malcolm,' he echoed, inflecting it differently, so that my name sounded much more important. 'Malcolm,' he said again, louder, so that the others could hear him, his open hand offering me out. My name was spoken up and down the table, with greetings and laughter, so that I couldn't be certain whether they were taking the piss or not.

When the drinks were served, the waitress put my beer down, then unloaded bottles of wine, disappearing for more. The woman to my left turned my glass over, and pointed the bottle towards it.

'Malcolm?'

'Oui, merci,' I said, getting my first look at her. In trying to keep my head down, she'd remained out of sight, and being so close, it was impossible to view her in passing – I had to turn directly to look at her. Her face was pale, without makeup, her eyes dark. As she poured my wine, I stared; her hair was longer than was fashionable, but cut so well, even I could tell she'd spent money on it. If it had been any darker, I would have said it was dyed. When the pouring was complete I said thank you again. She said, 'You're welcome,' in clear English, told me her name was Ameline, and breathed out on me, clean breath.

I checked for Herb's reaction, but he was looking to his left, into the mirrored wall. I followed his gaze until I found him staring at me in the reflection. He smiled, leaned closer to the glass, and blew on it, misting himself out of sight.

'Herb,' Ameline scolded, following it with French that was too quick to follow. Having been in Paris on and off or for six months, it was scandalous that I hadn't learnt more. I didn't get out enough, that was half the problem. The company was enjoyable in a way, but I felt a bit out of my depth, knowing nothing about them.

My food arrived, but having drunk some of their wine, I thought it was polite to wait for everybody else to get their food before I started. My seitan was cooked perfectly, sizzled around the edges, the baby potatoes oiled and coated in parsley. During the meal, Herb was silent, apart from letting the others know his food was good when the question was going round the table. When my mouth was full he asked how mine was, adding my name as a suffix to every sentence. Refusing to speak through my food I nodded vigorously, drawing my eyebrows together to show satisfaction.

'Bon?' he asked.

I nodded.

'Tres bon?'

I nodded, unable to keep my smile this time.

Ameline put one hand on my shoulder, and again spoke in English. 'Ignore him.' I expected her to go on, goading him, perhaps as their own joke, using me as a device to get at each other, but she went quiet, then took her arm away. When she spoke again, it was to me.

'Are you living in Paris?' she asked.

'No, I wish I was. Just visiting a friend.'

'Your friend is not here tonight?'

'No. He's not.'

'How long are you here for?'

'I've been here since May. I might be here a few more weeks. Maybe longer.'

'A long holiday.'

'Yes.' Somehow, struggling with simple English, both trying to make it as clear as possible, made this seem more poignant than small talk. Perhaps the broth of beer and wine helped, but I felt I was confiding in her, even though I'd skipped over the truth twice. It was so long since I'd talked to anybody apart from Claire.

Herb's food was gone already, making me sad that the occasion would soon be over. I wanted to talk more, but felt too self-conscious of my English, unsure how to take it further. A minute later, when the waitress asked if we wanted desserts, there was a general non, meaning we would be on the street in minutes.

They didn't even want coffee. Money was being pooled with
great efficiency, before the bill even arrived.

'Am I paying with you?' I asked Ameline.

'Yes,' she said, looking so startled, I think she thought I was
asking for a free meal. I pulled out enough Francs to match the
others, and handed them to her, rather than pushing them forward myself. A man who looked like an older version of Herb
– the same blemish-free skin – gathered the notes up and put
them into the saucer.

Following them out of the restaurant, I hung back a bit, to see
whether or not they noticed me. The air was even colder now,
the wind loud down the street. They were heading back into
town, sure of their direction, so I couldn't hang on any longer.
Herb walked ahead, joining the one who looked like his brother,
and Ameline had her back to me. I didn't want to draw attention to myself by saying goodbye, but felt stupid skulking off
without a word, so I started walking faster, to pass them. It gave
the impression that I too had a direction, and it meant I could
give a cursory wave before turning away.

'Where are you going now?' Ameline asked when I was
alongside, as we came to the main road, surprising me, because
I thought she'd forgotten I was there. The whites in her eyes
showed up more than the rest of her face, soaking in the halo-
gen drench from Notre Dame.

'Nowhere,' I said. I couldn't even add 'home', or say I was
going back to my friend's, because that seemed unacceptable
now.

'Are you coming with us?'

Before I could answer she stopped, and called for the others
to hold on. One of them looked back, but nobody even slowed.
She pocketed her hands, dipped her head against the weather.
Her hair was a mess now, but each time it got in her eyes, she
flicked it into the wind so it was dragged away.

'So?' she said.

'Where are you going?' I asked, not really caring, wanting to
say yes.

'Latitudes. Jazz bar. Do you know it?'

'No? But...'

She waved me to follow, then put her hand on my back to
speed me up, until we caught the others.

*

Drinking more beer was probably a mistake, but Ameline passed one back to me from the bar, and I didn't refuse. There's something wrong with my blood, which means I have to be careful about alcohol. It's not diabetes, but it may as well be. Eating vast quantities is a three-hourly requirement during the day (and sometimes at night), but I've got to go easy on refined carbohydrates and booze. One bar of chocolate can give me a sugar crash two hours later. My hangovers are only curable with large doses of pasta.

Although the meal sustained me, the caffeine from earlier left me jumpy and tired, so the beer was a welcome drink, calming my muscles while keeping me awake. I knew I was drinking too fast, but while the rest of the drinks were being bought and distributed, I had nothing else to do. The stage was between bands, and Ameline's friends had turned away from me.

When she was free of the bar, Ameline approached, carrying two more beers, which she held up to my face. Then she leaned close, and said, 'Shall we stay together?'

We seemed to have lost something in translation, but I said yes anyway.

'Wait for the music,' she said, her mouth so close to my ear her words were blown into it. 'Then we'll disappear.'

Her friends were dissipating towards the stage, taking up the few spare tables. By the time they were seated, the stage was lit up in blue, and the band found their places. It wasn't the sort of jazz I was used too. There were two thin men, playing trumpet and trombone, another on a keyboard (which doubled as a drum machine), and a black woman in a glitter dress. She appeared to walk on to stage with her eyes closed, and kept them that way for most of the first song. Her body was motionless, and her head only moved to accommodate the gaping of her jaw.

Ameline tugged on my shirt, and I followed her towards a table underneath the stairs. It was still crowded there, but we wouldn't be bothered by her friends. There was one long seat in the alcove, so we slid in together. She pushed a beer my way, tipped hers at her mouth. I must have been drunk by then, because I stared at her lips, trying to see her tongue through the lens of the bottle neck. Her face was sweating, not enough to drip, but giving it a definite coating.

'Will your friends mind?' It was wrong of me to bring this up, because I should concentrate on being with her, rather than worry about social etiquette. Her face was blank for a second, then she winced as though trying to find the right words.

'If we are broken up, we can meet again?'

'Why not? Yes. Are we likely to be separated?'

'Non.' She put her palms together, fingertips on her lips, then said, 'I don't want you to leave. You can come back with me, if we can.'

It was difficult to catch what she was saying over the noise, and the more she drank, the worse her English became. I had no idea whether she was inviting me back to her flat, or trying to make future arrangements.

'Where shall we meet then, if we are separated?'

'Do you know Luxembourg?' she asked.

'Sorry?'

Her face was blank again, either not hearing me, or not taking my meaning.

'Jardin de Luxembourg,' she said, waiting for me to nod understanding, even though I'd only passed through it once. 'In the park there is a café. It is close to where I live. We can meet in the morning.'

'If we are separated,' I added, drunk enough to be angling for a night time commitment.

With all this established, the conversation moved into standard form, me asking where she was born, what she did, what her surname was. She told me that her surname was Bayle, but I realised that I'd already forgotten answers to earlier questions. For minute I couldn't remember her first name, and found myself staring at the table, taking deep breaths, too pissed to carry on talking.

Below the table, she took my hand and stroked it. My fingers must have been cold, because they felt fleshless and bitter, her hands like hot towels working over them.

When I looked up she had gone. Opening my hand, I saw it curled against itself. The beer bottles had vanished, and I could only assume she'd gone to the bar again. I was losing minutes at a time. It's bad enough forgetting an evening the day after, but having it blank out while I was still awake was frightening and I knew I must slow my intake. My watch said that it was already past midnight. It didn't seem possible, and I struggled with the mathematics of the night, trying to work out where the time had gone.

A voice close to my ear asked if I was all right, in English. She was on the left now, and I tried to sit up straight, make my face alert and lively, rather than slurried with intoxication. The person sitting there was not Ameline, but I couldn't tell whether or not it was one of her friends. Her hair was much shorter, a muddy brown from what I could tell, but it was difficult to be sure in the blue light.

'Are you all right?' she asked again.

'Fine, fine, just tired,' I said, my breathing wet and raspy. 'Are you English?'

She blinked three times, rapidly. 'You are.'

I nodded, wondering how she knew. She must be a friend of Ameline's, or she'd heard us talking.

'Would you like to get out of here now?' she asked

I didn't reply, but wrinkled my forehead to show my confusion. 'I think I'm with somebody.'

She put her hand on my knee. 'Shall we stay together?' she said, and I noticed that I was so drunk, my eyes were rolling, vision rotating like a badly tuned TV, slamming down and down and down, so that I couldn't make out her face. It was almost impossible to hear what she was saying, and all I could tell was that she was speaking English, with a French accent. I put my elbows on the table and leaned over them, closed my eyes, but found that too dizzying, so stared at the rings of moisture left by the beer bottles, the water vibrating to the music.

For a while I thought I'd been sick, because my head was at the level of the table edge, spit winding from my mouth. It took great concentration to get through the sensation of spinning, but I knew that it would pass, if I could just hang on for a few minutes.

When I sat up I was alone, but Ameline was coming back to the table, Herb following. She sat by me again, Herb across from us. Another beer was put in front of me, this time by Herb, and I saw him mouth my name as he pushed the bottle closer. The two of them talked in their own language, so I sat back and tried to concentrate on the band, pretending it didn't bother me.

They stopped talking, and Herb leaned forward. He grinned and curled his fingers at me, to make me lean towards him.

After a slight pause, he said, 'Are you a twat?'

Sitting back I looked at Ameline to see her reaction, but she was watching the stage, as the band accepted applause, walking off.

Herb's smile was gone, and I thought that if I smiled – even nervously – he might hit me, so I looked down. Before they piped in more music, there was only the sound of conversation, made throaty with smoke. Ameline turned back to us, spoke to Herb in French until he shrugged, then she said to me, 'We are going now. Do you want to come with us?'

'With you?' I pointed backwards and forwards between the two of them, while Herb looked into the crowd.

'Yes. You can stay at mine.' She said it quietly enough for it to be a secret, but I still couldn't tell whether or not Herb was coming with us.

*

Blanking out as we walked, I got the impression we'd gone as far as the suburbs. Recognising a few street names, I knew we couldn't be that far out, but my legs were aching. Herb and Ameline were arm in arm a short distance ahead, while I dragged my feet, so cold I wondered if I'd discarded clothes along the way. My bladder was painfully bloated, but I knew they wouldn't hang on while I filled a gutter, and I'd be stuck on my own without a clue where to go. I decided to follow her home. If food was on offer, it would be wise to take it, and at least her flat would be warm. Most of all, though, I hoped she'd ditch Herb, so we could be alone.

The first time she spoke to me on the walk back, was as we approached a building, two stories high. She said it was her home, and climbed up what looked like a wooden fire escape which stank of varnish.

Inside we went into the kitchen. Herb pulled a chair out, and pointed it out to me.

'Malcolm.'

I said thanks as I sat, but he walked into the next room without a reply.

Ameline put a droplet-spattered jug of water in front of me, which was so bright in the neon light, I found it difficult to look.

'Wait here,' she said.

'Where's the toilet?'

She pointed down a hallway, told me to be careful, and went after Herb. The toilet at the end of the corridor smelt of bleach, and I had to kneel in front of it to aim properly. What could she be telling him, I wondered, as my bladder released a long gush. The flood was so fierce, my muscles stang in biting spasms, but it was a relief. Washing my face, I felt remarkably well considering the state I'd been in earlier. Knowing I should get hold of a baguette, I went back to the kitchen. No voices were audible, so I took a chunk of bread from a tray and chewed it dry, helping it down with water.

It didn't take long to drink the jug full, the pain in my stomach replaced with a mint-like cool. Kitchens are usually the coldest part of any building, so I wanted to go somewhere warmer, but stayed still when I heard the first noises. It didn't begin slowly or with caution, but in fast, grunting breaths from both of them. They must have been on a spring-free bed, or the floor, because there was no sound of movement, other than the distinctive scraping of skin on skin, and something wetter, slapping again and again. Herb was making sounds like a distressed dental patient, an open-mouth gurgle. Ameline was more high pitched, one note repeated over and over, so beautiful it would have been musical, if it hadn't been so monotonous.

It was so disappointing, I didn't even get a hard on. Not wanting to hear them come, and feeling sick at the thought of seeing them sweated up and smelling of each other, I left, closing the door slowly.

*

Against the glow of street-lit clouds, the Montparnasse tower looked like the black obelisk from *2001*, the few lights within reminiscent of stars. If I kept that to my back, I'd be heading north. I expected to feel terrible as the drink wore off, but my head was clear, and I didn't feel too cold.

By the time I reached Saint Germain, the edge of the cloud was peeling up, revealing white sky where the sun would be. The sound of litter moving over the pavement was unusually loud, making me realise how tired I must be. My hair felt sticky with smoke, so I knew I ought to get back to the flat, have a shower, see Claire.

Until then, I'd barely thought about her. It had been so easy to get carried along with the events of the night, that I'd hardly considered how she would react.

Rue De Bievre is more of an interstice between the buildings, than a proper street. Most of the people who live there have windows a car's width apart, and leave their shutters closed most of the time. The place where we lived was an offset cobbled courtyard, every balcony decked out with flowers, the white paint always new. It was normally a relief to turn off the draughty street, up our path, but I felt cramped in my stomach and nervous.

When I unlocked the door, I couldn't decide whether to go in quietly and wait, or to wake her. Perhaps I should get into bed. I opened the door quietly and saw that the shutters and curtains were open, which I hadn't noticed from outside. I went straight to the bedroom; again the shutters were open, the room freezing, because the window had been left open a few centimetres. The bed was empty, unmade from that morning. I checked all the rooms, but it was obvious she hadn't been back since the morning before.

The exhaustion was intense but I felt too dirty to sleep, and uncomfortable with the situation, so I closed the windows, undressed and showered. The water made so much steam, it was like breathing hot fog.

Before I was fully dry, I went to the bedroom to gather some clothes, but sat on the bed, so tired I had to close my eyes. I knew I should dry myself, because the drips on my back and legs were bitter, but it was difficult to resist sleep.

When I woke my towel was cast aside. The curtains were open again, the sunlight making my skin dangerously pale. It was nine o'clock. I didn't want to see Claire now, because even though I'd been with other people, I was annoyed at her for staying out. Dressing as quickly as possible, I left the flat without breakfast, glad to be outside again.

*

Although walled and railed around its perimeter, the Jardin De Luxembourg is spacious. Tree branches mingle into each other, but their trunks are set far apart, and the lawns between them are wide.

I walked up the footpath toward the main area, being dodged by a chain of joggers. More than a quarter of them were smoking as they ran. One woman, fully made up, hair in a tight bun bound with gold thread, minced in steps slower than I walked. Her boyfriend, wearing a long grey coat, followed at walking pace, having no trouble keeping up. She stopped every few feet, to catch her breath, adjusting the gold bangles on her wrists.

It was windless, but leaves fell continually. I always find it difficult to understand how a tree doesn't become bare on the first day of autumn. If it loses ten leaves a second, how can it stay leafy for over a month?

I walked around the circular lake in front of the white Palais. Many of the benches were taken, but I found a space and sat facing the sun. There was a girl further up, with a sketch pad. There's something attractive about women who can draw, that is impossible to ignore. This is probably why they do it, sitting in museums and galleries, sometimes cafés, pretending to sketch and observe. In reality, they are making you look at them, making themselves desirable.

She was drawing a man to her left. He was twice her age, and pretending he didn't know she was watching him. I could tell he was enjoying the attention, and wished she would draw me.

I watched birds flying over the water, a small child pushing its toy yacht around the edge of the pond. Further round, a couple were embraced on their bench, kissing with great open yawns. They rocked together, palms spread around backs. They stopped, looked away from each other as though shy, then moved back to kissing. I couldn't help staring, because I had never been with anybody like that. The warmth of seeing them together, so pleased to be kissing, never getting bored, no reason to argue, bothered me. I couldn't imagine being that close to Claire, or to any of the people I knew.

There was no point in putting it off any longer, so I got up and walked towards Rue Guynemer. Close to the edge of the park, I found the café, a wooden hut, painted black with green window-sills. It was too dark to make out people within; all I could see were the small lampshades on each table.

Inside, I sat facing the footpath to watch people passing, hoping I would see somebody I knew. What would I do if I saw Claire? It would depend who she was with. I'd probably sit there, hoping she'd go past. I didn't want to deal with it yet, even though it wouldn't be too difficult. I would have to leave, gather my belongings and make plans to be on my own. It would be a lot easier than staying.

The waiter brought me coffee with a plate of cheese and bread. Outside, a group of boys were throwing polystyrene aeroplanes. The white of the models was stark against the background of trees. They circled slowly, always flying back into the boys' hands, never colliding or stalling to the ground.

The girl with the sketch pad came in, signalled something to the bar, and sat on a nearby table facing me. She put her pad in front of her, flicked through the drawings until the waiter brought a dish of salad and a beer.

She knew I was watching and lifted her bottle, tilting her head on the side to stare into it. It wasn't fair of her to do something like that. She must have known I was vulnerable. I felt well fed, tired, warm, and she was doing this beautiful thing, blinking at her drink sideways, knowing I was watching, the light from the lampshade warming her face.

We looked at each other for a moment.

I wanted to spend time with her.

We could drink a couple of coffees, talking until the liquid dried in our cups. Then we would share a bottle of wine, and she would hold her glass carefully against her chest as she talked, before putting it to her mouth. It would get late, the café would close and they would usher us outside. We'd both want to stay, to spend more time together, but being nervous we wouldn't make arrangements. I wouldn't even walk her to the Metro. Walking home, I'd think about seeing her again, wanting to kiss her, my hands firm on her back. Picturing this would be as good as being with her.

My eyes were closing. Somebody spoke close to my ear. Where there had been a dryness in my mouth, I tasted charcoal. She said something about stillness, her breath warming my neck. I felt a hand in my own, and squeezed to make sure it was there.

When I opened my eyes, I noticed several things at once. The curtains were being blown open, held up by cold air. I was naked on the bed, across a damp towel, the hairs on my legs matted and soggy. I listened for sounds in the kitchen, the scraping of a chair, but there was only the wheeze of my own breathing.

I looked outside the café, and the children had gone. One broken aeroplane was being spread by the wind. It was clouding over, rain graining the glass.

The girl with the sketch pad had been joined by a friend. At first I thought it was the man she'd been drawing, but squinting to focus my eyes, I could see he was much younger. They were holding hands, their fingers never parted. Even when he used his hand to make a gesture, hers stayed within his.

What Happens Now?

As the train pulled out of Euston, the first sunset of winter made the passengers around me squint angrily. I couldn't understand their reaction. The past three months in London had been colourless, with air and sky a wheezy fog; the only colour came from street lights and dying leaves. Even those were polluted, looking more like jaundiced marzipan than the yellow they were supposed to be.

Passing one of the city's parks I focused on the trees, leafless and black, the sky behind them turning orange. It was going to be freezing, and I wondered how much heat Karen would be able to afford. When I visited her last, in June, her room was cold, giving the impression that it collected shadows even when it was sunny outside. She had moved further into the moors since. On the phone I asked what her house was like, and the word she used most was 'exposed'.

When the train left Milton Keynes, the sky became clear blue for the first time in months. As the stars came out, they were fuzzed away, presumably by mist. The fields were dark, all the towns distant. What little light there was glinted off an early hoarfrost.

It was a relief to be on the train, and although every other seat was taken, I spent the journey feeling pleasantly alone. The whole day had been spent reassuring Paula that my visit was innocent, that Karen was a friend, nothing more. She didn't get angry or slam doors, but kept asking about my past relationship with Karen, and why I was going back.

'She's just a friend, and it seems like the right thing to do.'

Handing me another cup of coffee, and sitting cross-legged in the armchair opposite, Paula said, 'So, why haven't I heard about her before?'

I wanted to get mad, but there was no accusation in Paula's tone, only enquiry.

'We haven't been in touch for a while. She rang out of the blue, and I said I'd go. It would be rude to say no.'

'Just like that? You drop everything and go just because she rings up?'

She was grinning, but it was the sort of expression that could quickly turn to a glare.

'I'm not dropping anything. We made no plans for the weekend, did we?'

'I didn't say we had. I just wondered why you jump to heel, the minute she clicks her fingers.'

'It's not like that,' I said, making sure I didn't get angry. Although I'd spent a lot of time with Paula in the past two months, she was a new friend, and I didn't want to let my temper ruin any trust we had gained. Even so, she should respect my past friendships, so I tried to explain. 'We've always had an unwritten agreement that if one needs the other, you know...' I trailed off, trying to work out what I was meant to be saying.

'So Karen needs you?' Paula asked, calm again.

'I don't know. She rang me up, asked me to visit her. I said yes. It's really that simple.'

When the train was dark, and there was nothing to look at but my reflection in the dusted glass, I wondered how simple it would be. Would I do this for anybody else? I couldn't think of any friends I would go to in this way, at short notice. It would be good to see her again, though, and that should be enough.

My eyes had gone out of focus with staring, and when I saw flickering I thought it was lightning. It took a moment for me to realise we were pulling into Wakefield station.

Walking up the platform my body felt achy and warm, in contrast to the frozen air on my face. Even though it stank of diesel, it was refreshing. Karen was sitting in the main waiting area, staring at the floor, and I couldn't decide whether she was doing that as an affectation – to look disinterested at my arrival – or because she was deep in thought. The fluorescent lights made her skin bluish, and her hair looked over-washed and brittle. She was wearing a long leather coat; I caught its smell, and then a breath of her perfume, before she saw me standing in front of her. When she looked up and smiled, vapour clouded from her mouth and I realised she must be a lot colder than me.

A hug, a kiss even would have been welcome, but there was no contact, and she didn't even say hello. Instead she told me that we should get to the car quickly. 'The windows were icing up all the way here,' she said. 'If we leave it much longer, we won't make it back.'

I slung my bag in the back of her mini and got in, positioning my feet amongst a debris of rags and crisp wrappers. She put a cassette in the stereo, assured me that I would love it, and turned it to a painfully loud volume before starting the engine. Her driving wasn't erratic, but she was distracted by the controls of her tape player. It was an ancient machine that buzzed and crackled; she reached behind it, apparently trying to rewire something, as we took the A636 out of town.

'It's snowing,' I said, when the first blobs of white hit the windscreen. Karen craned her head, unable to hear. I repeated it, wishing she would turn the music down. Instead she shouted, 'It gets worse the further out we go.'

The snow was made orange by streetlights, but this effect lessened as we headed into the hills, and the landscape became black and white. I couldn't read any of the road signs, because they were crusted and frozen. The snow stopped falling, but we drove into fog. I knew my eyes were tired, but I was finding it difficult to see more than a few feet ahead, and there were no white lines or pavements to go by. A stationary car could be just feet ahead of us. When Karen turned sharply to the left, up a banking, I thought she had skidded off, but we had pulled into her drive.

'You know the roads well,' I said over the music.

'Mmm?'

'You knew where you were going.' I exaggerated my mouth movements, so she could lip read, but she looked puzzled and nodded slowly. The drive went behind the house, and she pulled up, killed the engine, then the music and headlights. It was too dark to make out anything beyond the windscreen. The only sound was that of our breathing.

I climbed out, trying to get my bearings. The nearest streetlights were in the valley on the other side of the house, and if it wasn't for the gleaming snow, I wouldn't have been able to find my feet.

Inside, her house smelt of cold chip fat. I put my bag by the side of a chair and sat down, while she built a fire, keeping her coat on. It took her a long time, and I couldn't be bothered to offer help. It was exhausting watching her pile coal, bits of paper, finally shoving in cardboard. She made such a mess of it, I couldn't believe she had made one before. It smoked for minutes while she blew on it, and when it caught light, it only burned in patches, giving out no heat at all.

'That's better,' she said, taking off her coat, slinging it on to a bean bag. The room was a mess, everything appearing to have been put down without thought, including the furniture.

'Don't you keep plants anymore?' I asked, remembering the large, flowerless plants she used to own. She moved house five times while we were at college, and always dragged those things with her.

'No. I don't bother,' she said, looking absently at the window-sill, which was ornamented with paperbacks and coins instead.

'Did you get sick of carting them around?'

'No. I brought them, but there just isn't enough light up here.' Her expression changed to a wide smile, and she said, 'I'll make some food. You must be starving.'

I nodded yes, remembering why I liked Karen. She was the first person I spent much time with, even though we met when I was eighteen. I remember the first afternoon she came to my room, and I managed to make her laugh for hours. She was laughing because she liked me. I didn't sleep that night, amazed that I could hold somebody's attention, that she wanted to be with me, cared to listen to what I said. Karen used to make me look her in the eyes, and when I did she smiled. Sometimes she hugged me, and she was the only person I ever knew who told me I was a friend. Even lads I'd known for years, and girls I had been out with refused to use the word. Karen said it almost every time we went out; 'If we weren't friends…'; 'You're the only friend I can tell this to…' Every time she said it, I smiled inside. At the same time, though, the word was always a promise that nothing else could happen between us.

'It's just about ready,' she called from the kitchen, and I wondered if that meant we would be eating it lukewarm. 'It's just broth,' she said.

Having run out of candles, she put an angle-poise lamp on the table, and turned the strip light out. The food was more like yeasty water than soup, and was only potable when combined with chunks of bread. Karen kept scrunching her nose, making murmuring sounds, so she must have liked it.

'I suppose we could have some wine,' she said, and I realised how much of a struggle this meeting was.

'Yeah, why not?' I said, then immediately added, 'After a glass you can tell me what on earth I'm doing here.'

I couldn't see her face, because she was reaching behind the vegetable rack for a bottle, but she said, 'You're here because I missed you. We are friends. It would be silly to lose touch, wouldn't it.' When she stood up, her hair was all around her face, and she made no attempt to move it out of the way, but stared at me through it.

'Of course,' I said. 'But I was under the impression that you needed something specific.'

Karen placed the bottle in front of me, sat down again, and put her palms together between her thighs. She leaned forward, smiled, and said, 'I need you here. I appreciate you now.'

Unsure what she meant, I remained silent while she uncorked the wine and poured us an over-full glass each. It tasted remarkably similar to her broth, but I drank it quickly.

'The fire sounds like it's picking up,' she said. 'Let's get warm.'

I glanced around for a telephone as we went through.

'Do you mind if I call Paula?' I asked.

'Call her if you like. It's down there, by the newspapers.'

The phone was stuffed behind the armchair, and I crouched there, because I felt that sitting comfortably would look too presumptuous, as though I was settling down for a long call. It rang for a long time, and I kept thinking that if Paula answered, I would have to be careful what I said, in case I upset either of them.

'I don't think she's in,' Karen said after a while.

I let it ring a while longer, then agreed, and put the phone down.

'It's half twelve already,' I said, amazed at where the time had gone. I wasn't enjoying myself, and expected time to drag. 'I can't believe it's that late.'

'It's this place,' Karen said, looking at the curtained windows as though she could see on to the moorland. 'It eats time, which isn't such a bad thing, because you can't get much more lonely than this.'

It was only a matter of time, I thought, until Karen said something about us never being together, about it being a mistake. All her actions hinted that she wanted to be close to me now, in a way that went further than friendship. She was going to bring the subject up one way or another, and I wouldn't know what to say. Although it seemed more than obvious that she was going to say this, I knew it would surprise me, because it was such a contradiction to everything she had said in the past.

The first months of our friendship were agonising, because all the time we spent together was brightened by a pre-romance tension, which I knew was one-sided. After a party in February that year, I lay by her on the concrete floor of a garage, because there was no room left in the house. There was only one sleeping bag, and although I could easily have walked home, I eased as close as I dare, my back frozen and sore, certain that we would move together. She slept all night without stirring. When she woke she complained about the taste in her mouth and left, barely acknowledging me.

'You're out here by choice, though, aren't you,' I said, finishing my wine. I knew that comment might annoy her, but was surprised when her eyes filled, the thick tears fat with the light of the fire.

'I don't choose to be on my own.'

'Then do something about it,' I said as kindly as I could, putting my glass down. 'Move away. Find somewhere more hospitable.'

'Where? London?'

'I don't know. But look at you, Karen. You're obviously not happy. You have to do something about this.'

'I called you.'

Until that point her hands had been on her lap, making no attempt to wipe at the tears, but then she moved quickly, smearing the wet across her face as she stood and rushed across the room.

She was on me before I could react. At first I thought she was biting my face, because she was kissing me so roughly, and then her mouth was on my neck, wide, growing wetter, as her arms pushed me back into the chair, her nails digging into my shoulders. This only lasted a few seconds, and she was still, sitting on me at a strange angle. She was heavier than I had imagined, but this made her feel more substantial than she looked. Her proximity didn't annoy or distress me as I expected, and I allowed my hands to circle her back, moving my face into her hair.

While we sat like that, I heard something outside. It was like a chain being dragged to the rhythm of footsteps, perhaps a dog that had slipped its lead. The surprising thing was that it circled the house. Each time it went past the window, the chain clear and loud, I thought I could make out the padding of feet on icy ground.

'Can you hear that?' I asked.

'Your breathing?'

'No, that sound outside.'

She sat up looking at my face and said, 'I can't hear anything.' She got off me then and sat by the fire, hugging her legs as if cold. She stirred the coals with the poker and they reignited, the crackling loud enough to conceal the sound from outside.

I went to the window and pulled the curtains back, wiped at the condensation until I could see out. The small lawn was covered with snow, but the flags below the window were icy. I heard the sound again, just before the dog appeared. It was black all over, but its eyes must have been catching the light, because they glowed like amber. A chain from its neck dragged between its legs. It was much thicker than a lead, and three times as long. I watched the chain disappear to my right, then waited, wiping the glass clean as my breath re-misted it. When the black dog came back, it ran straight to the window and looked at my face. When it pulled its lips back over its teeth, it didn't seem to be snarling so much as smiling.

I backed away and flung the curtains shut, not sure how I could explain that to Karen. She didn't notice my sudden movement, or my shock, because she continued to stare into the flames. I didn't want to look out again, but I couldn't sit down and carry on a normal conversation having seen that. I knew if I brought it up, she would think I was changing the subject, trying to avoid what we had done.

'I'm going to bed,' she said, standing slowly. 'You know where you can find me, if that's what you want.'

She moved sleepily, lifting her jumper enough to untuck her T-shirt from her jeans. I caught a glimpse of her stomach as she left the room. There was no sound from the bathroom, and I guessed that she had simply loosened her clothes and gone to bed.

The fire was turning into cinders, and the room was already cold enough for me to see my breath. There was no more coal for the fire, and I knew it would be too unpleasant to sleep down there. I turned the lights off and climbed the stairs in the dark, convincing myself that at least it would be warm, and that was a good enough reason to share the bed with her. I could even tell Paula, in theory, and she wouldn't have to be angry.

There was one small window above the landing, which let in enough town and snow light to reveal three doors. I had no idea which was which, so tried the door to my right. It was the bathroom, and I relieved myself in the toilet, shivering because it felt like a refrigerated room, which smelt of crystalline chemicals.

The next door opened into a room that was big enough to be a bedroom, but was piled with clothes and boxes of books, leaving no floor space. The third door must be her bedroom, but when I reached the handle I stopped. A gap under the door gave no light. I didn't think she could have gone to sleep so quickly, but the darkness wasn't inviting. I couldn't decide whether to put the light on and talk, or just go in and get into bed with her.

Expecting the door to creak I was relieved when it opened without sound. I went in and closed the door, looking to my left. The bed was empty, but there was a circle of brightness on the duvet, coloured like moonlight. The black dog moved into the light, its fur shining so much it looked wet. Its eyes were like hot coals, and they fixed on mine. Without breaking its gaze, the dog barked, its head shaking with the effort, the sound loud enough to hurt my ears. The sputtering in its throat was so fierce, it almost sounded as if it was making words.

The curtains behind the dog were open, but the window was closed, the glass meshed with fine ice. I considered putting the light on, but although the dog remained stationary – its legs locked into position – it reached further towards me with its head, eyes growing hotter, more spittle running over its teeth.

When I reached for the door, the barking stopped, but I continued out and closed it behind me. I didn't have time to think about what had happened, because I saw light coming from the front room, even though I was certain I had turned it off.

I made a lot of noise going down stairs, because I rushed. When I opened the door I saw the fire, burning well, and sitting by the side was Karen, holding her legs, knees drawn up to her chin.

She looked up and said, 'Did you find it all right?'

'Find?'

'You found the toilet?'

'Yes.'

'Was it iced up?'

'No.'

'Sometimes it ices up.'

Using the coal-tongs, which had small brass hands on the end, she picked up pieces of coal and placed them into the flames. Then she left the room without speaking. I went to the curtains, pulled them apart, and saw that it was snowing again, the fog thinning out. Karen came back down with an armful of blankets, and a pillow.

'You can sort yourself out. You'll be better off on the floor, but don't get too close to the fire.'

She stood watching me make a bed out of the blankets, as though waiting for me to say goodnight, or give some signal that it was all right for the evening to be drawn to an end.

'Are you tired?' she asked.

'Yes.'

'Right. I'll get off then.' After a pause she added, 'I'm sorry about all this.'

'No, it's fine,' I said, not sure whether she meant my sleeping arrangements, or the way we had been together.

She shook her head. 'No, I'm sorry, dragging you all this way for nothing. You shouldn't be here.' Her smile was sadder than any frown she could have pulled. 'If the weather's okay, I'll take you back to the station in the morning.'

She turned the light out as she left, and I shuffled under the blankets in the glow from the fire, and waited. I had no expectation of sleep, and knew I would think about the dog all night, about the smell of Karen's hair, and the gurgling in my stomach from lack of food. I must have slept though, because my position shifted, and the curtains became blue. My watch said it was past eight o'clock, but I found it hard to believe I could have slept so long. My belly felt full, as though I had eaten. When I thought about making coffee, my stomach bubbled, and I moved back under the blankets, feeling cold and a little sick.

After a while I tried to ignore the sensation, and dressed, so I would be ready to leave when Karen came down. The sick feeling didn't get much worse, but the next time I sat up, my stomach protested with a cramping and I knew something was coming up. I didn't have time to reach the kitchen, so aimed for the tiles in front of the fire. My guts felt watery, but what came out was dry and black, crumbling like soil. There were strands of grass in it, and tiny stones. It was more like coughing than vomiting.

When it was over I was able to pick the stuff up and put it on the dead fire, which sagged and gave off a flurry of ash. I made sure the dirt was hidden, not wanting Karen to see what had come out of me, and then washed my mouth into the kitchen sink.

Karen came down in yesterday's clothes.

'Are you making a drink?' she asked.

'I will if you like. But I thought it might be better to get going straight away.'

She looked thoughtful. 'Yes, we could. We could go to Halifax. There's a market in the old hall.'

'I thought I was going back to the station.'

She sat on the arm of a chair and shrugged. 'If that's what you want. But I don't want you to go.'

It occurred to me that I hadn't thought about Paula in hours. Picturing her face, I knew it would be best to leave. I thought about getting back to the house, warming my body in the bath, maintaining the heat in bed with her. 'I think I'd better go.'

'You're certain?'

Her mouth pouted, going wrinkled like the lips of a long-term smoker. It was a peculiar expression and I couldn't help staring. It almost made me laugh, because I was feeling so much relief.

'Yes. I'll go.'

'Then catch a bus,' she said, without looking at my face.

I picked up my bag and went out before she had even moved from the chair, heading downhill, towards the main road.

Most of the snow had gone, a warm drizzle turning the hill-sides black. I could see the town in the valley, the buildings and chimney stacks clear. The sun was only a colourless circle at first, but as I walked, it warmed.

I remembered the last time I went to the Lakes with Karen. It was the third week in April, and it snowed every night. Each day was spent watching the white melt, trickle and eventually dry with a few hours of late sunshine. On the last day we went for a walk, talking so much we lost track of where we were, ending up by a small lake I'd never heard of. She became quiet, and walked ahead of me. I trailed her as she moved from place to place, surveying the surface, dipping her fingertips in the water, wiping them on her coat. Her back was to me the whole time.

The memory made me frown, and looking up I saw the main road. I knew that I would find a bus stop before long, and that Karen wouldn't pick me up or come running after me. She was probably sitting in the same position, wondering when I'd go back. The sun over the town brightened, the clouds pulling apart around it, and I remembered something else about that time by the lake. Karen had muttered words I didn't hear and kissed my cheek. I couldn't tell whether her lips were hot or cold.

Looking back, I realised there was something other than her contact that bothered me. Like so many other evenings, the sun was setting, the blue light on her face was turning yellow. I wanted to hold her, and all she did was walk away.

Despite the Cold

The sky darkened past blue before they reached Salcombe, and Stuart knew he wouldn't get to see the coastline. The last time Tim picked him up at the station, it only took twenty minutes to drive in. That was a couple of years ago, and no doubt the landscape had changed. The van was older too, its engine sounding rough and too sharp at the same time.

The Devon countryside used to be a flow of cereal crops. Now it looked like they were growing vines of some kind.

'I can't tell where we are,' Stuart said lamely.

Tim adjusted his glasses, brushed his sloppy hair aside and peered forward. 'Hardly know my own way around,' he said softly. 'It's always changing. You won't recognise the old town, Stuart.'

'That's okay, it's good to get away from London. I'm always grateful.'

'Not at all. You're always welcome. You'll get to meet Rosie and Helen this time. Good people.'

It didn't matter that he would miss the sea. Ever since he was twelve years old, Stuart looked forward to meeting new people. Rosie and Helen. One of them could be her, he thought.

Stuart was never at ease being driven through Salcombe. It was built on a bowled hill around the harbour, its buildings crammed together at every level with tiny alleys the only routes. Tim drove as though there was room for normal traffic, the suspension chattering over cobbles.

As they turned a corner, the headlights passed over something metallic at the side of the church wall. It was a scattering of long, silver things; they looked like dry fish.

'Quiet tonight,' Tim said. 'It's just the dark. People stay in. And of course we don't have tourists now.' He stopped the van and they climbed the stone steps to the veranda of Tim's hotel; it was difficult to see, because there was only one street lamp nested in the leaves of a rowan tree.

The Terrapins Hotel reminded Stuart of Christmas, even in August. It was a small building, with room for five guests, and felt more like a family home. He only ever stopped there during Tim's holiday, which must have maintained the illusion. There wasn't a lobby, only a desk in the corner of the main lounge. The bulbs in the lace lampshades were different colours, giving the impression of a nightclub that had seized up, with shreds of light frozen on to surfaces.

Stuart touched the cream piano, glad that it was still there. Its keys were painted garish colours, most being yellow, orange or blue. He wanted to sit down and play a few notes, but resisted for the sake of silence.

Tim dangled a room key in front of him. 'All yours, when you're ready,' he said. 'I'll prepare some nourishment soon. Come and meet the others.'

Stuart pocketed the key and followed Tim to the bar. The tables were round, covered with golden plastic, the shelves stuffed with plants and black ornaments. Tim went behind the bar, facing a woman on a stool.

'Stuart, this is Rosie, Rosie, Stuart.'

'Hello,' Stuart said. She didn't look round, but shifted her body on the stool until she was facing him. He could only see her right eye; the other was covered with a patch, taped down over cotton wool.

'Hello, Stuart,' she grinned, friendly enough now. 'Sit down,' she said, though he could barely hear her.

'Why are you whispering?' he asked.

Rosie pointed through to the dining room, but he could only see tables, and the oak alcove drifted with netting.

'I can't see...'

'That's my friend Helen. She's having a little cry.'

'Is something wrong?'

'She has sadness. Caught it when we first came here a couple of weeks back. There's a lot of it around. She'll be over the worst in a moment. It comes in waves.'

Stuart looked into the dark room again, but still couldn't make anybody out.

'Right then, drinks for the people,' Tim said, his arms out again, indicating the bar.

'Oh thanks, anything you suggest,' Stuart said, taking the next-but-one bar stool from Rosie.

Tim held each glass to the light, before pouring the iced gin. There were four glasses. The last one must be for Helen.

Stuart tried not to look into the dining room, but he was attracted to its dimness. He expected her to wander through, looking dazed and worn out, but she had composed herself quite well from the look of her stature. She wasn't tall, but her back was athletically arched, so that she didn't look small. Her hair came forward around her face, and strands were wetted on to her cheeks. She made no attempt to hide her crying.

Tim introduced them, but neither said a formal hello.

'Sorry for being so antisocial,' Helen said. 'It's this bloody… sickness.' He noted that she avoided the word 'sad'.

'Gin, good,' she said, taking a large gulp, holding the glass against her lips for sipping.

Rosie put a hand on Helen's back, her one eye closed. Stuart couldn't tell whether she was trying to heal her, or whether it was an expression of despair. One eye wasn't enough to tell by.

He could smell Helen's perfume, like elderflower. It reminded him of somebody else, somebody special, but he couldn't think who. The scent was so startling that he almost asked her what it was, but resisted, in case it was simply the smell of Helen's skin, with soap and deodorant.

Already Stuart felt he could enjoy being with these people. Rosie's face was tanned, not from sunlight, it appeared, but from wind, the outdoors; an even wood-coloured tan, rather than redness. Although Helen wasn't pale, she didn't have that worn appearance.

'Anybody getting towards food?' Tim asked.

The seating arrangements were something that bothered Stuart. He couldn't decide yet who he wanted to sit next to, but if he left it too long, he would have no choice. He was careful not to stare. His watching could easily be taken as lechery. Rosie moved sharply, her walk more of a trot. She slid round the back of the table, and Helen joined her, lowering on to the seat so slowly that she appeared to be aching. Stuart wanted to sit next to her, but instead he moved round to sit next to Rosie. He blushed, because he had done something stupid, and it was too late to move now.

'I'm honoured,' Rosie said, putting her fingers on his arm for more than a second. He tried not to flinch, but was certain his muscles fattened for an instant. To cover it he smiled, and tossed his head back with too much laughter. No matter how many first meetings he looked forward to, he always messed them up like this, overacting. He breathed deeply and adjusted his cutlery.

While they waited for the food, Rosie asked him questions: how did he know Tim, how often did he come here, where did he live, what work did he do. It was familiar talk, but he enjoyed it, making sure he answered to both Rosie and Helen. Then he asked the questions back, again to both of them.

When Tim came through with bread rolls in a wicker basket, he said, 'Not long now folks,' in a whisper. Usually it would be an announcement, but their conversation was so flowing, Stuart could sense that Tim felt like an intruder.

'I'll give Tim a hand,' Rosie said. 'I don't want him to feel like our servant. Look after each other.'

For the past ten minutes they had been talking constantly, a sequence of enthusiastic interruptions, all three eager. As soon as Rosie went into the kitchen, Stuart found himself struggling for words, and Helen looked down at the table. She leaned forward on to her elbows. He tried to think of something to say, but he was so desperate not to mention her illness, that he couldn't bring himself to ask anything.

'Are you here to convalesce as well?' Helen asked, still not meeting his eyes.

'Sorry?'

'Are you here to recover?'

'I suppose I am. I didn't realise. I mean, I thought you were ill since getting here…'

'The sadness?' Her eyes were on his now, wide and no longer red. 'Yes, I caught that a few days ago. Sad about nothing, but sad all the same. It's no fun, but it will pass.'

'So, there's something else. That you're recovering from?'

'Yes,' she said. 'Something else. And yourself?'

'I don't really know. Yes, I suppose. I have a problem with my memory.' Already he wanted to explain to her, tell her what he knew, in case it reminded her of something, but he became nervous when he heard the others coming back.

Tim walked carefully, trays and plates balanced on his arms. Rosie tiptoed behind, holding a pot of pasta that must have been too hot for her, because she nearly threw it down.

When Tim had checked that everybody was happy, and they had settled into the food, Rosie turned to Stuart and said: 'So, what were you two talking about?'

It surprised him, being so direct it was almost rude.

'Illness,' he said, struggling to swallow a sun dried tomato, and a mouthful of bread.

'Ah.' Tim gave a long, repeated nod.

Rosie pulled a face of incredulity, then smiled. 'So soon? We're not even drunk yet. We're showing our age, you know, talking about our ailments all the time.'

She's going to ask what's wrong with me, Stuart thought, hoping she wouldn't. He needed more time. It wasn't something he discussed at all, not even with Tim, or friends in London. He wanted to explain it to Helen, but not yet.

'I'm so pleased you three are here,' Tim said, 'but it's really not the best place to come for a recovery. The town isn't well.'

'Since the commercial change?' Stuart asked.

'Well, that's changed the look on people's faces. And we get more sadness here than most places. But there's other things going on. Too many complexities spreading through the countryside. Black helicopters come down the valley most weekends, spraying that yellow goo. Didn't you notice that nobody paints their houses white any more? No point, because they end up yellow.'

Stuart stopped eating. 'The spray's to simplify things?'

'The spray just kills flies. They can all spread complexity, even if they're not biters. It's a bigger problem out here than anywhere.'

'But there will always be flies,' Helen said.

Rosie wagged a finger. 'I think the yellow spray is fly food,' she said, holding her wine glass up, as though toasting her statement. 'I think they're breeding better flies, to pass the stuff on faster.'

'Always one for a conspiracy theory, our Rosie,' Tim said. The two of them fixed mock grins at each other.

'Forgive us,' Rosie said to Stuart. 'We like to play.' As she said it, she put her hand on his arm again, and this time he did move. 'You've got a touch taboo,' Rosie observed, the pitch of her voice rising.

'No, no, you just surprised me.'

She put her hand back on his arm, and he moved again.

'There, see, you have,' she said. 'Is that what's wrong with you?'

'No, not really.'

Helen smiled for the first time. It was the sort of smile that made Stuart want to smile back at her, but she was enjoying his reaction, so he let the worry stay on his face.

Rosie saw he was staring at Helen, and touched him again as a distraction.

'You're flinching. I can see we're going to have to cure you of this.'

Tim's face contorted through humoured approval and veiled discomfort. It was more like empathy than sympathy, Stuart guessed. Rosie had probably put him through similar public embarrassments.

'I'm going to leave my hand on your arm for a while,' Rosie said, firming her grip.

'How will you be able to eat?' Stuart asked.

'The things I'll do for you,' she said. Then her good eye closed, in a long, slow blink. He guessed that it was a wink, but with no other eye to judge her expression by, he couldn't be sure.

Helen refused to look up now, and he wanted her to see that he wasn't happy about this, that he didn't like being touched by Rosie. When she put her knife and fork down, he thought she was going to leave, excuse herself for the night and disappear. It was a relief when she said, 'I think we need more to drink.'

'Yes, barman,' Rosie said, scrunching her nose up at Tim, 'serve us more drinks.'

'As you wish,' he replied, bowing his head.

While Tim opened more wine, Stuart tried to convince Rosie to let go of him.

'I think I'm cured,' he said.

'Really?'

'Yes, really.'

'So I could touch your face, and it wouldn't bother you.'

He pulled back as her fingers reached for his cheeks.

'No,' he said, holding a hand up. 'But that's different. There aren't many people I would allow to touch my face.'

'But some?' Helen asked, her smile back, taunting him.

'Well, sometimes.'

He thought she was still laughing, because she lowered her head, but then he saw liquid soaking into the tablecloth. He knew there were tears when she started sniffing, wiping hands over her eyes, though her face was hidden by drooping hair. Rosie put a hand on Helen's back again, letting go of Stuart at last. Tim sat with his hands in his lap, not speaking, then bit the end of his thumb.

'I wish there was something we could do, Helen.'

'No, it's all right. It's passing now.'

She was quite out of breath, her face lined with tears that she spread with the sleeves of her top.

'The worst thing about all this,' she said, 'is that I'm not sad about anything. These aren't my emotions. It's just directionless sorrow.'

'Would it help if there was something to be sad about?' Stuart asked. He was trying to be helpful, to sound caring and perceptive, but thought his statement was flippant.

'It would help, yes,' she said, with a last sniff. 'Imagine being in love, and not knowing who you were in love with. It's like that. When it hits me I feel terrible, but for no reason. If I was sad about somebody, or an incident, it might help.'

'Well, drink up,' Tim said, not sounding too hopeful.

If she was this bothered by an infection, Stuart wondered what her real illness was. He had only ever had two doses of sadness, several years ago, and both were minor. They came to him at times when his resistance was low, after splitting up with girlfriends, so the sadness seemed fitting.

Rosie stuffed her nose into the glass and breathed. 'I don't know what I'm doing,' she said, her attention on Stuart, 'I don't have the first clue about wine. I just know it's more chemicals.' She took a swig. 'Mood in a bottle.'

'Good mood or bad mood?' Stuart asked.

'Oh, perfect mood. It never does me any harm,' Rosie insisted, scratching the side of her eye patch. 'I won't get violent on you or anything. But it's a false mood, don't forget that. It's as false as Helen's sadness. It's happiness about nothing.'

Tim and Helen both kept their glasses by their mouths, and he couldn't tell whether they were hiding smiles or frowns.

Stuart took a largish gulp of wine. 'I don't think that's fair. The mood is genuine. Booze makes you happy, sadness hurts. The feelings are real.'

'Oh yes,' Rosie nodded quickly, 'but they don't mean a thing.'

'So, if we have a good time on wine tonight, do we have a good time or not?' Stuart asked.

Rosie touched his arm. 'Of course we do, but it's not genuine.'

'I don't know what that means,' Tim said, 'What does genuine mean? If we're happy, we're happy.' He grinned with his teeth showing, which was unusual for him, and seemed to be an attempt to prevent the discussion turning into an argument.

Stuart interrupted the flow, his eyes moving between the three of them. 'When you're tired, that mood is brought on by chemicals, isn't it. Your brain loses its balance, and you're in a bad mood. It's still your mood.'

With a waved hand Rosie dismissed this, a strained frown over the single visible eyebrow. 'No Stuart, the difference is that these chemicals,' she swilled the wine glass, 'come from outside of us. To be genuine, the mood chemicals should be made by us. If I'm sad about something, my brain makes sad chemical. It's a symptom. An effect, not a cause. What Helen has, what we're drinking, are symptoms.'

'It hurts just the same,' Helen said. Then she smiled, as if to say it was okay, she was only joking.

The first bottle of wine was gone already, so Tim brought two more through, with a corkscrew. He apologised for being a slack barman, and made reference to his mouldering bones. It was only a light comment, but Stuart noticed they were all red with laughter, which must mean they were getting drunk.

As if to confirm this, Rosie suggested a toast – a symptom of the intoxicated. Stuart didn't even hear what the toast was, because when they raised their arms to tap their glasses, he was shocked into silence.

'What's that smell?' he asked. 'Something sweet,' he said when the others stared at him. It was like wheat after rain, and made him smile involuntarily.

'Probably me,' Helen said, with a look of guilt, as though he had said she smelt of shit.

He wanted to tell her it was beautiful, but knew he couldn't without embarrassing her further. She saw that he was struggling, and shook her head, mouthed the words, 'It's all right,' and he mouthed, 'I'm sorry', still not sure what was going on.

After that he went quiet again, though everybody made a point of making sure he listened to them. They weren't mad, and for them the embarrassment had gone. His mind wandered, thinking about this, and he must have lost the conversation, because Rosie touched him again 'You're dying to look aren't you?' she said, fingering her eye plaster.

'Yes,' he said, not sure whether to agree or deny it.

'I'll show you mine if you show me yours,' she said.

Tim left the table with a groan. Helen pushed her chair back and followed him.

'Show you what?' he asked.

'Tell me what's wrong with you.'

'I have something wrong with my memory,' he said, realising that he wanted Helen to hear about this, wanting her to come back. Perhaps his show of honesty would make up for his blunders earlier on.

'Do you forget things?' Rosie asked, looking disappointed.

'No, I remember things that never happened.' Even while drunk, the image came back to him as he talked. He was in a long room lined with books, on the second storey of a large house. The books were held into the wall with golden wire. Outside the window a sunset melted behind leafless trees. And somebody was with him. He could never see her face, but knew what it would be like to be with her. 'It's just pictures and thoughts. Feelings. It's difficult, because I care about people I've never met.'

He heard piano music, something simple, repeating. Helen was working the coloured keys, and he wanted to be in there, wanted this conversation to end.

Rosie was barely moving now, in contrast to the jumble of limbs she had been earlier.

'Where do the memories come from?' she asked.

'I was infected by somebody else's RNA. It was after the first laying-down drugs came into use. When they tried to cure people of their past, the memories took flight as transfer complexes. It's rare, something they simplified within a few weeks. I was unlucky. Probably caught it from an insect bite. It's embedded now, and I can't forget it.'

He drank more, and she spoke to him in response, but her words meant less and less, growing quieter as the sound of the piano increased. For a moment it seemed that Rosie was singing the notes.

Tim was in the same room as Helen, laughing. Then Stuart found they were all in there. He was so drunk that he was plunging into blank sections, unaware of how he was getting from one place to another. Scared of what he might say, he went upstairs.

Stumbling to his knees in his room, without turning the light on, he thought about the things Tim had said as he left. There had been a joke, and something about black dogs. Tim told him told to watch out for black dogs. He didn't realise he was being sick until the vomit was out of him, a hot trickle dripping over his lips as he lay down.

He stared at the chunky puddle until he slept.

His skin was numb when he awoke. The weather was warm, but the window channelled breeze over his skin. A pale stain in the carpet reminded him why he never made it to the bed.

After a quick shower he went down, and found the others arranging breakfast pots on the table outside the front of the hotel, under the rowan tree. Everybody said good morning, but not much else until they had eaten for a while. Tim occupied himself by providing enough food and drink to keep everybody quiet. Stuart shifted round on the stone bench, so that he could shade the sun from his eyes with the rowan tree. He could see its berries now, just forming as black silhouettes, though he knew they must be rouge.

'Do you remember your dreams?' Helen asked.

It was a general question, and the others nodded, making agreeing sounds, but nobody elaborated.

'I remember mine,' she said. 'And they change things. If you dream about somebody, it doesn't matter that it wasn't real. It changes the way you feel about them.'

'Have you been having secret dreams about me again, Helen?' Tim asked.

'Timothy,' Rosie said, buttering more toast with rapid knife strokes.

'No,' Helen replied, 'but if I did, would it make a difference? I think it would. If I dreamed that I slit your throat, I'd feel uncomfortable with you. It doesn't matter that nothing actually happened, I would feel different.'

'We're all waiting,' Rosie said, and when there was no response, she added, 'For you to tell us who you dreamed about.'

'I dreamed about Stuart of course. I'm sorry, because I barely know you.'

'Don't worry, I don't feel invaded,' he said, delighted, but also baffled by the fact that she was telling this to everybody. 'Was it a good dream?' he asked, again wishing he had kept his mouth shut, because it was too private a subject to ask about.

'It was confusing. No offence, Stuart, but I think you represented somebody else. You were a face stuck on to an emotion.'

It was too early in the morning for a conversation like this. It would have gone down well last night, but Stuart could see that nobody was happy about it. Even Helen looked like she would rather be silent again, and her shoulders sagged.

Tim offered to give them a tour of the town, to see the changes. They locked the hotel, and set off down Buckley Street, curving their way downhill towards the sea. Tim said they would have to take new routes, because of a piping system through the town. He pointed this out, down the next alley. The pipe was taller than two people, coloured black, its sides pressed against the other buildings.

'There are five like that, all coming from the sea. They've knocked down so many good buildings to put these pipes through.' He pointed out derelict buildings, where families had moved on. 'They could have changed the pipe routes, and knocked the empties down, but took the shortest route instead. We lost the library and the post office, and one of the churches, though the graveyard's still there.'

Tim walked ahead, his stroll making him less hunched than usual. Indoors he tended to lean over, to disguise his height, but outside he lifted his head and led the way, the others asking questions, knowing he enjoyed giving a show.

When they reached the sea, it was surprising to see it so

clearly. In the past the harbour had been choked with boats, so that the sea was merely suggested. Now there were only two maintenance boats, with orange lanterns on their roofs. The sea itself was clear, apart from a mulled, pinkish colour beneath the surface. After watching for a while, Stuart could see the colours were laid in strips. At the edge of the harbour, the five pipes met, arcing into the water.

Tim took them to the edge, and pointed out the rows of squid.

'They're based on a standard squid design, you can see by the round suckers, but the brains have been bred out.'

'They still have eyes,' Helen said.

'Yes, but they're not conscious to any great extent. We don't think.' Tim sounded unsure. 'You can only just see the tubes; there's a catheter from each, which takes the ink to the main pipe over there, and sucks it away. The processing plant is behind the hill. The pipes are a problem, but it's better than having the factory down here.'

The squid looked like plants, apart from their eyes, which made Stuart uneasy, because they blinked.

'Do they all make the same colour?' he asked.

'We export black and blue inks. There are ink farms all along this coast for the other colours. Apart from red, which tends to be grown around Newcastle, in odd places near the copper farms.'

'It stinks,' Rosie said, pushing Tim's back, urging him to move on.

Stuart could smell something other than the squid, something more like cooked cabbage, but he didn't want to comment about smells anymore, after upsetting Helen. They walked through a scattering of dead fish, which looked dry, their eyes black holes. They weren't rotten, but scales lifted from their bodies in the breeze, like silvered flakes of skin. There were seagulls above, and he couldn't understand why they weren't taking the food.

Heading back up the hill towards the town centre, he saw another pile of fish. They were also dead, but fresher, the eyes plump and the scales shiny with slime. Nobody else noticed, so he didn't mention it.

Tim led them down an alley so narrow they had to walk single file. One of the pipes went overhead, supported by arched wooden beams. Passing underneath it felt cold, and he couldn't tell whether that was because of the shadow, or some quality of the pipe. Beyond it, Tim turned up a path towards a house. He announced that it was the secondhand bookshop, and Stuart could see the windows piled with browned paperbacks.

Inside, the light was the colour of weak tea, the glass stained as though they had been coated with old sellotape. Most of the inner walls had been removed, as well as the first floor, making it feel more like a large hall.

There was an electrical, fizzing sound. The bookshop owner was standing behind his desk with a plastic fly-swat, striking the buzzing creatures that crawled around his window.

Stuart headed down one of the shelf-corridors, pretending to look at books, hoping he would bump into Helen. The book-shelves were arranged like a maze, so that the further you went into them, the darker it became. At first the smell of dust, which stank like dry ashes, made him breathe though his mouth. When his lips went dry, he breathed through his nose again. He could smell something like tree sap, and heard the floorboards creaking. His eyes hadn't adjusted properly, but he could tell it was Helen when she came round the corner, by her outline.

'Okay?' he asked, whispering more than was necessary.

She stood in front of him, but then turned so that her back was facing him. 'Smell my neck,' she said, tilting her head forward.

He put his face close enough to feel the heat of her skin, and breathed, trying not to sound like he was sniffing. Without real-ising it, he put his hands to his mouth with surprise. He couldn't place the smell, but it reminded him of something that he wanted. He wanted to hold her, kiss the taste of her skin.

'Do you know what's wrong with me?' she asked, her voice so quiet he struggled to hear.

'No.'

Helen turned round, no smile on her face. 'I can never hide how I feel. My emotions are transferred into scents. If you know me well, you know what I'm thinking, because I stink of feel-ings.'

She backed off a little, leaned against the bookcase with her eyes closed, head back. Then she opened them wide and white, looking at the ceiling. Stuart's sight had adjusted, and he could see dust falling into her eyes, but she didn't blink.

'My emotions are too rapid,' she said, shrugging. 'I don't know who you are, but in my dream, you were with me. That's why I smell beautiful today.'

She said sorry and walked past; he felt sure there couldn't be room for her to pass without her chest pressing his, but she shuffled against the books, and made it through without contact. The smell was more like grass now.

He stayed there, letting her scent be replaced by the thick odour of books. He could hear other voices, all whispers. There were people nearby, but he wanted to be left alone.

It was an impossible situation. If she was attracted by a dream, and he was attracted by a scent, there was nothing genuine, no real reason for them to like each other. He doubted that she could fit in with the memory. If she didn't then eventually he would be restless with her, as he always was. This annoyed him. It was childish, he thought, to cling to a person he had never met. He resolved to forget the images, to forget the room, and the person who was there. It wasn't his memory. The woman could be dead, or married by now. It might not even be a real memory; the one who passed it to him could have been dreaming. He wanted to let go of it, but even as he made the promise, he knew it was something he could never suppress.

He was annoyed, and ran his finger along the books in front of him, trying to be interested in the titles; the sound of slow feet on the floorboards bothered him, because he was constantly trying to work out which was the sound of Helen.

One book made his finger stop. He pulled it out, examined its black cover, and the picture of a female, blurred and drifting, melting across the page. He tried to open it, but his fingernails came away from his right hand, bloodless. The book fell, and he examined his fingertips. The skin had receded, melded into nubs of bone. He screwed his hand up to hide it, and headed out of the shelves.

Rosie and Tim were waiting outside, sitting on the wall.

'Helen's not well again,' Tim said, 'she made us promise to let her go back alone.'

'We're going back now anyway Tim,' Rosie said sternly.

'Yes, we'll go back.'

Stuart walked behind them, uncurling his fist to examine his hand. It had stabilised, the finger ends like glassy chalk. He knew he had to stay calm, or the complexity could spread. Salcombe wasn't a stable place any more, and was bringing out the worst in all of them. If their patterns went mobile, they could push the town beyond its catastrophe limit. His hand was evidence of that. He promised to stay away from Helen for a while, to let things become normal. They could meet again, away from here, in pairs, not as a large group; the effects were obviously worse when invalids were brought together.

He was the last to get back to Terrapins. Helen was in the dining room, her arms folded on the table, hiding her face. Rosie was by her side, calming her, so he knew it couldn't do any harm to approach for a while. Her crying wasn't violent, but fecund, the tears matting her hair. It smelt like seaweed.

He sat down with them, enjoying the calm, until Tim came through.

'Tim, stay away,' Rosie snapped.

Tim put his hands on his hips. 'I'm not doing anything, Rosie. I only want to help.'

Helen's crying was audible for the first time. Stuart wished she would look up. If she could see his face, that might help the sadness, if he could show that she hadn't upset him, that he was pleased about her.

'Tim, I think you should back off for a while.' Rosie's face was a mixture of pale and red; the anger draining her and making her flushed at the same time. Stuart expected a protest from Tim, but he left without another word.

'I don't know what's happening,' Stuart said, unsure whether or not he should leave.

Rosie left Helen in place and sat back, scratching at her temples. 'It shouldn't be like this. Not today. Is there a surge?'

'I don't know,' Stuart replied, wondering if she was referring to the local entropy.

'Are you infectious?' Rosie demanded.

'I don't think so. I don't know. I don't know what's happening.'

'The problem with this place,' she said, gritting her teeth, 'is that we're all in love with each other for no reason.'

Her face went stiff with pain, the tendons in her neck enlarging. She pressed one hand against her eye patch, then hooked her fingers around it. It came away with a ripping sound. The flesh in her eye socket was dull, her eyelids raw. Moving closer he saw that the iris had changed shape, the pupil appearing to have been dragged through it, threading a black trail into the white. The veins around it were harsh, feeding into the dark area, making it fat. It twisted around itself, as though flexing a spine. Her cornea was swollen with fluid, and the tadpole swam there in tight circles. She tried to blink over it, but there wasn't enough skin to close the lids. Its fidgety movement continued, turning to violent wriggles.

There was a sound like rushing air, and a bang from outside. It was followed by another rushing hiss, another sharp explosion.

Helen stopped crying, sitting up to listen, but didn't wipe her face. 'Flares,' she said. 'Something's wrong.'

Helen ran out and thumped up the stairs. Rosie's neck appeared to have lengthened, because she was straining so harshly, and her head was bowed. She didn't seem to have heard the flares. Her lips drew back over her teeth, and she made tiny coughs.

'Are you all right?' Stuart asked. There was no reply, so he told her he was going upstairs, and ran. He could hear wind, and knew the other two must be on the balcony in Tim's room. It was on the fourth floor, and his lungs were stinging when he got there.

The light had changed. The sky was the colour of sea, thick, fast-moving clouds as low as the far hills. Tim and Helen were standing in the rain, both looking to the right, staring at the hillside above the town.

'What's happening?' Stuart asked, struggling to make himself be heard, his shirt and hair already wet through.

'The season lost its grip,' Tim said, pointing at the highest trees on the northern hill. They had yellowed, the leaves advanced by a month. They went brown and fell together. The wave of yellow spread down the hill, hitting trees as though bleach had been poured over it.

It felt as if there was sand in the wind, but Stuart realised it was ice. A door slammed below, and Rosie hobbled down the steps, into the street beneath them. She was using the wall to hold herself up.

'Where's she going?' Stuart demand, but nobody answered.

It was difficult to tell how far the effect had reached, because there weren't many trees in the centre of town, but looking down they saw the rowan tree lighten, its leaves crackling and falling. Even at this height Stuart could make out the berries, because they were swollen.

Rosie stumbled again, her left leg giving way. Something silvery trailed out of the leg of her jeans, the material going thin. She fell and shrank, her clothes going flat as fish poured from them. The street was wet and sloped downhill, so the fish splashed into the gutter and swam down it like a stream.

There was a smell like burnt sugar. Stuart looked back to the bony trees. The wind pushed fallen leaves down the streets, into drifts like brown snow.

Over the water, seagulls were trying to fly in formation against the wind. In unison, they dropped, their wings slack as they plummeted. There was no noise, only foam where they hit the surface.

He wasn't sure if Tim and Helen had seen this, so pointed, but they only looked at his hand. The flesh had withdrawn as far back as the joints, the fingers now curls of bone. They were supple for a moment, then set. He stuffed his fist under his left arm, to hide it and keep it warm.

The three of them stayed on the balcony for a long time, despite the cold. The rain stopped, and the wind dropped, though higher up it was strong enough to rip the clouds, letting sunlight through.

When Stuart felt that he was beginning to dry off, Tim moved away. 'I'd better get Rosie's clothes out of the street, before dogs get to them,' he said.

Helen was damp, her T-shirt solid on her body. He looked at her neck, and tried to breathe its scent. She smelled only of rain. He put his good hand on her shoulder, where the skin was cold. He kissed her neck, then tasted his lips.

She turned, moved towards him, her face pushed warmly against his, her arms around his back.

'Anything?' she asked.

'No, not yet.'

'Don't worry,' she said. 'It will come back.'

Something About Tomorrow

Pia never spoke to Julian much, and when she did he expected that it would be for a favour. She collared him in the corridor outside Michael's room. It was too narrow for people to stand opposite, unless they enjoyed each other's breath, so she stood next to him, leaning against the cork-board.

'Busy?' she asked, pulling breast pads out of her leotard. She bent towards her bag, unrolling a bundle of clothes and a towel. Pia was one of the weaker dancers, prone to fatigue and injury, one or both ankles adorned with snap-bandage. Every time she made a false move, she would gasp, as though trying to hide her discomfort, but hissing loudly enough so that people were aware of her pain. Pretending to be brave, she was usually being the opposite.

'Just waiting for a word with Michael.'

'You could go in,' she said, wrinkling her nose, sniffing. 'He won't mind.'

'He's on the phone to Beryl.'

'Anyway, I want to ask you something.' She buried her face into a hand towel, stretching the skin on her face as she dragged it away, giving him time to think before she spoke again. 'In magic, how do you make something appear from nowhere?'

'You don't. You make it appear from somewhere. You just make it look like it's appeared from nowhere.'

'So, there has to be a source for something? Nothing can just come into being?' The fingertips of her right hand were gripping those of her left, and she looked off to the side, visualising something.

'No, of course not. Why?'

As she dressed, putting on jogging pants and a cardigan, Pia explained that a small bird appeared in her flat each morning, even though she kept all the doors closed. 'It's been going on for two weeks now. It must be coming from somewhere, mustn't it?'

'I could have a look if you like.'

'I'd appreciate that Julian.' She unclipped her hair, ruffled the worst of the creases away, put on glasses, rounded up her bag, and raised her eyebrows. 'Coming?'

*

Julian's work at the theatre was part-time in terms of pay, but he spent more time developing effects for them than anybody else. His ad remained in *Yellow Pages*, offering illusions for theatre and performance, but the only people to show an interest were the ballet company. That was down to Michael. When they met, Julian was doing restaurant work to supplement his income.

He never enjoyed performing, because of the image that magic carries with it. No matter how good your effect, you come across as a grinning berk, out to fool people with a silly trick. If you perform well, people think you're an idiot for spending time practising something so futile. That's why he never bothered to become a stage magician. Instead he worked on the technical side of things, inventing new principals, applying old ones in new ways, pushing himself into theatre. Still, table-hopping at The Dilshad restaurant on weekends brought in enough money to feed him, and it wasn't as though much of a performance was expected.

His audience was always limited to four, because the restaurant didn't attract larger bookings. It smelt of cumin, coriander and fat. The decor consisted of red curtains and gold lights, which made it dim enough for him to get away with some really crap effects, like the floating match. There was one night near Christmas, when that completely threw one bloke. 'I'm an engineer,' he said, scratching at the cold sore on his bottom lip, 'and I don't know how the fuck you're doing that.' The match was floating over a gimmicked card, held up by a cross-hatch of 'invisible' thread. One of the cheaper Tenyo tricks.

Restaurant magic had gained in popularity over the last few years, and by hiring Julian and a couple of others, the Dilshad knew they could attract more customers. They tended to be couples on a first date, pleased for a distraction, something more to share than food and uncertainties. They were also the most eager to be happy, trying to impress each other with their capacity for joy, which meant they enthused over everything he did.

Rainy evenings were best, because they put people in good moods. Coming in from the rain must have made people feel cosy, warm, something like that. There weren't so many bad punters, trying to catch him out. Julian's tack was to play it straight. Rather than trying to make them laugh or flourish his way to applause, he would simply make a space for his case while introducing himself, asking their names, and would then perform without expression, letting the effects do the work. If handled cleanly, that should be enough.

To gauge a table, he would perform his weakest trick first. This way, if they were busy in conversation, they would make it clear that he wasn't wanted, before he wasted time on anything difficult. It was the first trick he ever learnt; passing a coin through a pen. Basic sleight of hand. You throw the coin past the pen and catch it. A swift jerk of the fingers makes it look as though it's gone straight through. People are more willing to believe there's a trap door in the pen or coin, than the dexterity of a human hand.

Michael was the first customer he'd come across who was sitting alone. He didn't look as though he was expecting anybody, which meant he might have come out to be on his own. The last thing he'd want was a pushy magician. The Dilshad was quiet, so Julian had no choice but to approach him once he'd ordered. The man looked up, his eyes white against tanned skin. His hair was so black it must have been dyed. Everything about him suggested a hurried attempt at faking good looks, in contrast to his genuine smile. His expression was so warm, Julian hesitated, wondering if they knew each other.

He ran through his basic patter and asked for the man's name.

'I'm Michael. So what's this for?'

'Just entertainment while you're waiting.'

Without saying anything else, Julian held up his 2p, pressed his pen into the tablecloth, moved the coin against it, then passed it through.

Michael thought for a moment.

'Could you do that again please.'

'A good magician never repeats his tricks,' Julian said, feeling uneasy, especially about calling himself a magician.

'Please,' Michael said, making eye contact.

'All right.' As he pressed the coin against the pen, Julian saw that his fingers were shaking. He made the pass, relieved that the coin didn't fly out of his hand.

'Could you use an ordinary coin for that?'

'Oh yes. In fact, do you have a pound coin I could borrow?'

Unlike most people, who struggled to help him with this one basic request, Michael delved into his inside pocket and withdrew a fistful of change, spreading it on the table.

'Take your pick.'

Selecting a quid, Julian switched it with a prop pound coin, and placed the end of the pen against its centre, then pushed it in, the length of the pen disappearing through the centre of the coin. There was no sleight here, nothing fast or deceptive; the pen just went through the middle and rested there. You were meant to perform this with a cigarette, but there was no smoking in the restaurant, and customers didn't like to be reminded.

'Wonderful,' Michael said, but his expression was so tight, he looked angry.

With another switch, Julian returned the original coin, which Michael examined, stroking it as though feeling for Braille.

'I'm sorry to interrupt,' Michael said, as Julian opened his Bicycle card deck, 'but can you float objects?'

'Yes, small objects,' he said. It was perfect timing. The floating match card was stacked at the back of the pack. He held it a few inches from Michael's face, placed a match on top, flexed it to make the thread taught, and the match rose. He plucked the match from the card, and struck it on top of his case, letting it burn down, to show that metal and magnets weren't involved.

'I wonder,' Michael said, looking down, 'whether you can float something larger.'

*

At first it meant working nights. Julian insisted on being alone until the illusion was perfected. If people saw how he set it up, they wouldn't be able to tell whether or not it was effective. He wanted to treat the dancers, technicians, everybody as though they were the audience. The theatre was in use all day, which meant he could only come in after midnight, working until dawn.

The effect Michael asked for was simple. As the curtain went up, three dancers would be standing inside a large, translucent box, painted with the outlines of trees. The box would rise above the dancers, and hang motionless, floating, with no sign of wires. Although he wasn't seeking dramatic magic, he didn't want people to be distracted from the performance, and wires would cheapen the whole set. This approach suited Julian, even though the allocated budget was tiny.

It wouldn't be difficult to disguise wires, if he was able to put in a black or shimmering background. Sequins on cloth would be perfect, but the set designer said the background had to be plain, like a cinema screen, lit in varying shades of blue and copper. Hiding wires in plain sight wouldn't be easy.

For the first three nights, Julian worked on reducing the bulk of the box. It had been built by somebody fond of pine, plastic, metal and glue, although it made more sense to use slotted bamboo doweling, with the painted material stretched around it. The box was still too heavy to be lifted by standard magic threads, and anything thicker would be seen in the front twelve rows.

'Are we winning?' Michael asked on the fifth morning, his face still squinting with fatigue.

'It'll be ready on time,' Julian promised.

'Right.' It was usual for Michael to get the facts then disappear, but this morning he stayed put, pushing his lips out in a thoughtful pout, scowling at the stage floor.

Julian ran his hand along the edge of the box. 'I'll move this out of the way then.' Michael didn't reply. 'So you can get on with rehearsals.'

'Are you very tired?' Michael asked.

'No, why?'

'Come with me for breakfast.'

Michael took him to a café three streets away, perhaps for privacy, or because he favoured the place. He led Julian to a table by the window, pushed the ashtray aside and sat with his fingers locked, breathing towards the glass, his breath thickening there as mist. The café smelt of steamed fish, and the tables were glazed with the wiping of damp cloths, smeared crumbs and ketchup.

Julian felt nervous, not sure what they could talk about or why Michael had asked him out for breakfast. The silence made him think something was being demanded. Perhaps his pay was going to be lowered. It was possible the lighting people were getting sick of him, always asking for more lamps to flare the background.

'Do you eat hash browns?' Michael asked, as the waitress came closer.

'I will do.'

'The usual please, and the same for,' he paused, 'for Julian.' The waitress was already heading to the kitchen. 'Julian,' Michael repeated under his breath. He touched his eyebrow, scratching it with the fingertip rather than the nail.

'I suppose this is your supper, isn't it. Thoughtless of me to put you to bed with a belly full of fat.'

'I'm not sleeping much at the moment. I'll be up until lunch time.'

'Right.' Michael didn't appear to be listening, so Julian launched into an explanation of his plans for the box, explaining how he was going to use Kevlar, a type of carbon fibre. It could be stretched into a thread so slender it was almost impossible to see, but could still hold the weight of an elephant.

'I need to talk to somebody Julian,' Michael said, looking directly at him, sitting forward over his elbows.

Julian blushed, but before he could speak the breakfast was served. Apparently forgetting the weight of his previous statement, Michael smiled at his food and tucked in, using his fork like a spoon.

To Julian, the hash browns tasted of salt and margarine, with a hint of potato.

'What do you want to talk about?'

Michael stopped chewing, his eyes locked on to the plate.

'I'm surrounded by people every day. I talk all day.'

Julian ate slowly, taking small bites, so that he wouldn't finish first and be left with nothing to do. For the rest of the meal, Michael was silent, only looking out of the window when he lifted his coffee to swill down the food. When the hash had gone, they replaced their knives and forks in unison. Michael put money on the table, and they left.

'You're going for your tube?' Michael asked, pointing towards Aldwych.

'Yes, I'd better get back.'

'Can we do this tomorrow? I need to talk. I'm having problems with some of the dancers. Don't breathe a word will you.'

'Problems?'

'Women,' he said. 'I try not to, but. Tomorrow.'

He waved as he said that, turning his back, which was as close as he'd get to saying goodbye.

*

Eating Ricicles at six in the evening, Julian tried to convince himself that it was morning. The windows were closed, but he could tell that the sunny air outside was frosty. It was one of those days where the sky is so clear the aeroplanes are magnesium sparks, leaving no vapour trails. It felt like dawn, rather than dusk; all that spoilt the illusion was the sky going dark as he watched.

His left eye twitched and he rubbed it, knowing that the perversion of his sleep pattern must be doing something to his nerves, even though he felt alert.

In half an hour, the room was cold and full of streetlight. If he breathed with a wide mouth, making H sounds, he could see his breath as orange mist. Julian's hands were patterned with the shadows of the net curtains, and he closed his fists, aware of pain in his knuckles. When autumn was in full swing, his chilblains would be back, the pain of the blisters made worse by handling brass close-up props. By Christmas his fingers would seize again, putting him out of work. He rubbed them for warmth, but the pressure only drained the tips pale.

A brown mini pulled up outside, the occupant turning his headlights to sidelights before getting out. It was Michael, and he looked up and down the street as he walked to the door. The living room windows bulged in front of the house, so Julian was able to see his front door from the breakfast table. Michael rang the bell, and Julian considered sitting in the dark, ignoring him. They were only a couple of feet apart, but with no lights on he couldn't be seen, and the house would appear empty. Michael brushed his hand over his mouth and chin, then patted his solar plexus as he waited. He blew into his hands, looked at the window, rang the bell again.

After a second, he took a step back, about to turn, and Julian rushed to the door, turning lights on as he went, so Michael would know he was in.

The hall light made Michael screw his face up.

'Hi. You've left your lights on.'

Michael didn't look back at his car, but stepped inside.

'I won't be stopping long. The battery's fine.'

He waited for Julian to point him into the front room. The sofa and the armchair were quite a distance apart, which made talking difficult, but it felt more natural than sharing a chair.

'What are you doing on this side of town?'

'Just driving,' Michael said.

'Do you want a drink?'

'No, I'm going to be driving.'

'A brew?'

'No. I'm glad you're up. I thought I might find you in bed.'

'I'm hardly sleeping. I've been up an hour.'

'It's cold in here, Julian. You should put your heating on, or get out more.' Michael rubbed his hands together. 'I'm going to drop a few packages off. Review material, press photos. Just driving round town, dropping things off.'

'Oh. They're managing without you then?'

'No performance tonight. You could go in earlier.'

'Yes, I could.'

'I'll be up late, I suppose,' Michael said.

His face had the set of somebody standing in a queue, trying not to look impatient.

'I could come with you,' Julian offered.

'Yes, yes, you could. If you want. I mean, if you want to, you can. I could drop you at the theatre afterwards. It's up to you. I'll just be driving around.'

'Yes fine.'

'Right then.'

*

With the heater on full, Michael drove them into town. The footpaths were dull with frost, even though the air was made sharper by it. The mini wasn't fitted with a stereo, but the scrape of the engine made it difficult to be heard. Instead of talking

Michael pointed out things that interested him.

As they passed through Wood Green, by the abandoned scaf-folding of the market, Julian could see a fight. There was some-thing about the violence, he thought, and its style of movement, that made it detectable even when it was impossible to see what was going on. The same applied to drunkenness; all personal style of movement was eradicated, replaced by a clichéd slouch. In this case, the people were both drunk and violent. Two thin men pushing a fat skinhead. He was so pissed he couldn't lift his arms. Their punches were pathetic, no more than swinging slaps, but the fat bloke kept fixing his face on to the end of them.

Michael braked for the lights, affording them a clear view.

'Lock your door,' Julian said, securing his own.

'It's nothing to worry about. I used to live behind that mar-ket. Bought my lunch there every day.'

By now the skinhead's face was blacked out with blood, only his teeth and eyes distinct.

'They're giving him a good kicking,' Julian said.

Michael's face went green as the lights changed, and they pulled away. The fighters were still at it, giving Julian the impression that having run out of ideas, they were repeating the same movements.

'I hate seeing things like that.'

Taking more short cuts than direct routes, Julian began to see London as a series of narrow alleys and awkward junctions, lanes running behind warehouses and shops. Occasionally he would spot somewhere he recognised, such as The Conservatory bar, reminding him that he was in the centre of town.

Every few minutes, Michael would pull over, leave the engine running, and run off to a doorway, stuffing a padded envelope through.

'We're on double-yellows,' Julian warned, after Michael parked on a curb so high, it felt like the car might tip over.

'Just drive off if anybody comes,' Michael said, with an encouraging smile.

'What about you?'

'Come back for me.'

Never having driven in London, Julian didn't fancy escaping traffic wardens or the police, trying to find his way back to

Michael. He locked the driver's door while waiting, even though the street was empty. There weren't enough lights to see far, and that made him nervous.

When Michael was back in, he dipped the clutch, released it again without selecting a gear and sat with his hands on his lap. Julian tried not to look at him, pretending this was normal behaviour, until Michael said, 'We could go back to my flat for a while, if you have time to kill.'

*

For the first hour Michael busied himself around the flat, changing CDs, brewing fruit tea, passing Julian copies of *Dancing Times* with relevant reviews in, even washing up at one point. As soon as one task was achieved, he would find something else to distract him.

'I'd better be getting into work soon, if that's okay. It should be finished by the time you get up.' Michael looked blank, so he added, 'The box.'

'You're going in now?'

'Yes.'

Michael shook his head. 'We're a little out of synch aren't we? Well. Do you want to get changed?'

This was probably a reference to the fact that Julian was wearing yesterday's clothes. This was a new habit, something he wasn't particularly proud of, but it was practical. No point in putting clean clothes on as soon as he got up, because by the time he set off for the theatre, hours later, he would be grubby.

'I should, but I don't have time to go back really.'

'I'll sort you out.'

There weren't any cupboards, so Michael's clothes were hung and packed into spaces which resembled bookshelves in the hallway. Julian expected a long process of being offered various garments, but Michael gathered his choice up quickly and held it out to Julian; shirts and jeans that looked more like Julian's than his own.

'There's plenty of hot water,' Michael said, nodding his head towards the bathroom. 'You can shave with my razor if you like. The new blades are on the window-sill.'

'I dry shave. Wet shaving irritates me. I come up in a rash.'

Michael mimed shaving, hacking at his face. 'You do it like this, tearing at the skin?'

'Well.'

'You're doing it wrong. Long, clean strokes. '

'Oh.'

'Do you want me to shave you?'

Julian felt tired. With the curtains closed, lamps lit instead of overheads, and the music becoming quieter, Michael's flat was toning down for sleep. It was confusing Julian's pattern more than usual, and shaving for work might wake him up.

'If you're gentle.'

The bathroom was so small, the sink overlapped the bath, and Julian sat on the edge, while Michael filled the bowl. He renewed the blade, washed his hands, made Julian tilt his head back, and pumped Gillette gel on to his palm, rubbing it into lather. Smoothing it on to Julian's face and neck, his fingers didn't make contact with the flesh.

The echoey sound of the bathroom and the proximity of their faces, made them talk in whispers. 'One stroke for each section,' Michael said, resting the blade below Julian's sideburns. He drew it down swiftly, dipped in the sink, and repeated this three times. 'That's the left side done. The secret is to use a new blade every day.'

He held Julian's face at the chin, gripping with thumb and forefinger, repeating the movement on the right, then on the neck. 'Always shave downwards,' his said, breath warming on the freshly scraped skin. 'All done.'

When Julian looked at his face the foam had been removed, but his skin felt soapy and slick, stinging with chemicals. As he rinsed in cold water, he watched the whiskers spiralling down the plug hole.

Michael turned the shower on, testing with his fingers for a good temperature, and the room filled with vapour.

*

At Julian's side, Gavin worked the lighting controls manually. Although the company owned a computer that could drive the lighting desk, he preferred to time the mixing by hand. 'Otherwise I'm just an electrician,' he explained. By using his hands each night, Gavin could add artistry, and improve his performance with time.

Julian wondered if that observation was a dig at him. The illusion rigging was built with touring in mind. When the company set off for the provinces next month, Gavin would be left in charge of the illusion, which meant Julian had to make it simple to store, transport, set up and operate. When it came down to it, all Gavin had to do was flick a switch.

The stage looked a long distance away when seen from the lighting gallery, and Julian wished he could watch from the stalls with the rest of the company. There was nothing he could do up there anyway, other than sit back and let Gavin do the work.

The curtain went up, revealing a plain background glowing with rose.

'Dawn rising,' Gavin said, fading up five controls with splayed fingers. The background became yellow, brighter, mixing briefly into olive green, then blue. As it cleared towards white again, Gavin started the tape and the music began, layers of chords held for seconds at a time.

Using taped music saved the company thousands of pounds, even though it was frowned upon by some reviewers. It was essential for the majority of their work – the modern dance – but when used for the crowd-pulling classical sections, it had limitations. A tape couldn't respond to dancers the way a conductor could, but it was less temperamental than an orchestra. 'A tape machine's more flexible than the sodding MU,' as Gavin put it.

Gavin scratched his head, the shaved scalp making a crunchy sound under his fingers, and shook his body from side to side, nodding, the way people involved with a Walkman do.

'You ready?' he asked.

'Yes, go on.'

On stage the tree-painted box moved off the ground. There was no wobble or pendulum effect, no sign of wires. Miniature motors were built into the rigging, making the frame vibrate each strand of Kevlar. You could barely see the stuff at two feet away, so by vibrating the wires they were made invisible. The servos slowed the box gradually, so that it came to rest without a jolt, fifteen feet off the ground, apparently floating.

Gavin opened his mic on to the PA channel, announcing, 'And so on,' to the stalls, before raising the house lights, blacking the stage and stopping the music.

'You off?' Gavin called, as Julian stood up.

'Yes.' He was annoyed, but didn't want to look as though he was trying to get away, so said, 'Did you think it was all right?'

He shrugged, resetting his controls. 'Yeah.'

'I'll show you how to set it up later.'

'No, you're all right. I can manage.'

*

Throughout the first dress rehearsal, Michael sat alone in the fifth row. He acknowledged Julian with a stiff wave, which was his version of a thumbs up. Julian joined the dancers in the wings, helping them to time their entry into the box, co-ordinating with Gavin according to pre-curtain light fades. Unable to see the wires, they were nervous of breaking them, but it worked without a hitch. If they were worried about the box falling on to them, it didn't show.

When it was over, Julian went looking for Michael, but so did everybody else, seeking opinions, advice, a slap on the back. Michael lost himself somewhere in the building, but the word was that he'd enjoyed it, and it was typical of him to go quiet at such times.

In the back corridor, Julian spotted Michael heading for his office.

'I've been looking for you,' Michael said, his tan flushed, eyes tired. 'Here.' He passed a folded note to Julian, made an excuse about a phone call, and went into his room, locking the door.

The handwriting was neat, rather than hurried. It said, 'Let's go out tonight. I'll pick you up at nine. Well done.'

*

The front door opened into a dark space, like a squat corridor that gave access to the other rooms. Pia's flat must have been prepared for a visit, because the floor was free of the plates and clothes that usually decorate the homes of dancers. Even her newspapers were stacked next to a box of empties.

'Wait here,' she said, going into the bathroom and closing the door.

Through the door he heard her undress, put on the shower, and climb in. She breathed against the water, then dropped the soap. As she bent to pick it up the sound of water spraying the bath increased, then softened as she lined her body into its flow.

From where he stood, it was difficult to tell which was the living room and which was her bedroom. He didn't want to go into the wrong room, because if he was caught trying to get out, it would look bad. He could stand in the kitchen, stare out of the window, get a drink of water, anything other than wait where she had left him.

By the time he decided to head for the yellow room, which was catching the most light, the water was turned off. He took a step towards the yellow room, but the floorboards creaked, so he stopped. He could hear her towelling skin, pulling on clothes.

Pia came out barefoot, wearing jeans and a sweatshirt, angling her head back as she raked fingers through her hair. She didn't look at him, but said, 'Just a second.' In the kitchen, she took a couple of Belgian beers from the fridge, snapped the caps off, handed him one, and went towards the yellow room.

'Come on.'

He followed her in. It was the bedroom. She sat on the armchair in the corner in a line of sunlight, leaving him to sit on the edge of her bed.

'Drink up.'

Pia played with the stereo – never letting go of her drink – putting on a New Age tape, something with flutes and triangle, so quiet it was irritating. She sat crossed legged in the armchair, drank some of her beer and grinned. The sunlight made her look sweaty, even though he knew the damp on her face was probably from moisturiser. Although her hair was wet, he couldn't help but see it as greasy.

They talked about work at first, Pia complaining about the strain Michael's choreography was putting her under. 'I can't,' she said gesturing upwards with her hands. 'He stretches us to the limits. For a while he had this obsession with collapsing the body. Now he wants to go the other way. We're stretched.'

He asked her about ballet school, the demands of touring, and waited for her to ask about his life. While she brought more beer for herself from the kitchen, he talked about magic, and the effects he was planning. It was a surprise to find himself enthusing to her over the instant quick change he was working on. He would fit the dancer with loose fitting, opaque clothes, over a second, brightly coloured costume. The dancer would kneel, and as she stood, a hooking winch would drag the clothes off and through the hole in less than a second. To the audience it would look like the first outfit had vanished.

He was about to go into more detail as she settled into her chair again, but she said, 'Can you show me something magic now?'

In a way this request was a relief, because at least he wasn't boring her, but he said, 'I don't generally carry props around with me.'

'Oh come on,' she smiled. 'You know you want to. I can lend you a pack of cards.'

He stopped her with a raised hand, knowing how difficult it would be to work with somebody else's mangled cards. He was also worried her enthusiasm might be a mask, and that if he showed her something simple, she would laugh. In his back pocket he separated his Unique Coin, a pound and a penny, and put them on his right palm, curling his fingers to urge her closer. Without closing his fist, he shook the coins, and the penny disappeared. It looked like expert sleight of hand, because he never covered the coins, but it was all down to a precise use of magnetism and milling.

'Well then,' she said, looking at his face (giving him the opportunity to ditch the gimmick), 'you'd better find my holes for me.'

The search didn't take long, but it bored him, and he found himself out of breath. He was frustrated at being unable to solve the problem, but too tired to bother about working on it properly. When he came back into the bedroom Pia hadn't moved, but she looked different. This was perhaps more to do with the sun going in than her expression.

She finished off her beer, put the bottle down, and picked up three juggling balls. They were the bean-stuffed type, made from red, yellow and green material. She threw them up one at a time, uncoordinated.

'It's good for stress,' she assured him, then put them down again. 'Did you find anything?'

'There's a space behind the wall in the corner, where there used to be a fire. In the front room? It could be an open chimney. It's possible they could be coming in there, but I don't know how they're getting out of the wall cavities.'

'If you don't believe me just wait and see,' she said, smiling with her bottom lip forced against the top one.

He wanted to leave. By staying on all day for dress rehearsal, he'd worked well into his sleep time. He explained this to Pia, saying he would need to sleep soon if he was going to reorient himself.

'It's up to you,' she said. 'I can't force you to stay.' Her voice sounded cross, but she looked so sad he felt a misery for trying to leave.

'I'm going out with Michael tonight. I've not slept since this time yesterday. Longer. I'll have to sleep before I go out.'

'There's a bed if you want it. I'll keep out of your way.'

He was tempted by the prospect of sleep, rather than another half hour on the tube home.

Pia wouldn't look at him now, even when she said, 'I'll call Michael and tell him to pick you up here.'

When he agreed, Pia took his beer bottle from the floor and started drinking it herself.

'You get some sleep,' she said between gulps.

*

It was dark when he woke, only the radiator visible where orange light came under the curtains. The duvet was warm, but his nose and lips were cold.

Pia was in the room, crouching by the bed, pulling at the covers.

'One's coming through,' she said, moving closer.

He hadn't slept enough, because his mind was still swinging with dizziness.

'One what?'

'I can hear a bird coming through.'

'Give me a minute.'

'Hurry,' she said, grabbing his hand, urging him out of bed. She didn't give him time to get dressed, so he followed her in his boxer shorts, heat lifting from his body

'Why are the lights out?' he asked. The curtains were open allowing streetlight in the front, where it spread on the varnished floorboards, giving him enough definition to see by. Pia didn't answer, but shushed him and said, 'Listen.'

Behind the wall, something was scratching.

'Should we wait to see where it comes through?' he said. 'If the others have made it through, I don't see why this one shouldn't.'

'It should be out by now,' Pia said.

The scratching was replaced by wings flapping against a surface. It gained some height, then fell, paused, tried again.

'Is there any way we can unscrew the panel?' He felt around the edge, but it was sealed into place. Answering his own question, he said, 'No, if you want to free it we'll have to knock this through.'

Pia left him there, crouched in the dark. It was raining outside, so he hugged his legs, pressed his lips against his knees, wetting the skin with his tongue. He hadn't done that for years; it was something he used to do in his room at home, when he was thinking; partly for the pleasure of their roughness, but also for the taste.

Pia returned with a wooden tray of hammers, spanners and screwdrivers.

'Do you want me to?' he asked, but she said no, checked that the head of the lump hammer was secure, then slammed it against the plaster.

'Should I put the light on?'

'No,' she said, hitting the wall again.

The movement inside stopped, making Julian worry that she had knocked it senseless. Beneath the plaster there was hardboard, and Pia reached in behind it, pulling it down. It snapped at the top, and she kept pulling it away, so that she was surrounded by debris, her hands white with brick powder.

A starling flew from the dark space, heading for the window, its wings marking the air with dust. It hit the glass and dropped, but continued flying at the window, trying to pass through, its neck bending with the effort.

When it gave up, resting on the sill, Julian went closer. Its body was doubling in size with each breath, beak wide, the tiny needle-tongue lifting. He opened the window, and the bird flew back into the room, then returned, flying past him and out.

With the window closed he turned on the light. Smeared with dirt, on her knees, Pia was staring into the hole. There were ashes in the fire, fallen bricks, and around these, bodies of dead birds. Their feathers were gone, the skin like bat wings, pulled dry over a lattice of bones. On each eyeless head, there was an open yellow beak.

*

From the back seat, Julian leaned forward to hear Michael and Gavin talk. Their voices were loud, but the strumming exhaust beneath him made it impossible to discern their conversation. Gavin turned round, laughing, so Julian assumed he must have missed a punchline. He smiled for the sake of solidarity, but Gavin rolled his eyes.

'Are we late?' Gavin shouted to Michael. It was the loudest thing he'd said all night.

Michael didn't respond.

'Wrong side of town,' Gavin said.

Julian felt guilty, then annoyed, because it made no difference whether they picked him up at Pia's or his own. Besides, he hadn't even known Gavin was coming, and didn't welcome him. They wouldn't have been late in the first place, if Michael hadn't gone for Gavin beforehand. In an attempt to pretend he wasn't phased by this, Julian said, 'Where are we going then?'

There was no reply, so he tapped Gavin's shoulder, who looked round halfway, then forward again.

When they stopped at traffic lights, the engine noise softened, and he said, 'Where are we heading?'

'Not far,' Michael said.

Becoming annoyed, Julian said, 'Where exactly,?' so loud they couldn't pretend not to hear him, even as Michael revved up.

After a pause, Gavin shouted, 'Fulham,' then talked to Michael, his voice inaudible.

The space in the mini was minimal, so he couldn't see past the men in front of him. The road appeared to be on the edge of a park, but the side windows were fragmented with rain, so he couldn't tell. Michael pulled up outside Chapel Lafayette. 'You two go along, I'll park.' Gavin dipped his head as he got out, and lifted the seat for Julian.

'There you go mate,' he said. Perhaps the prospect of spending time alone with Julian was forcing him to be polite. Or it could be that Julian was projecting his anger on to Gavin, overreacting because he hadn't expected a crowd. It could be that he just didn't know him, wasn't used to him.

'Crazy driver,' Gavin said, when Michael drove away.

'I hadn't noticed,' Julian said, then added, 'Yeah,' forcing a laugh.

The bouncers of Chapel Lafayette both wore thick moustaches, which could have been bought at a joke shops. Inside, most people drank from bottles rather than glasses. Overdressed, they flouted their wealth via bolt-sized earrings and glossy haircuts. Michael would fit in here, and Gavin could get away with it, but Julian felt scruffy.

'We're drinking Red Needles,' Gavin said, pointing at the bar.

'I don't drink that sort of thing.' He wanted to say that he didn't drink at all, but now it sounded like he was being awkward.

'You'll do as your told.' For the first time Gavin produced a friendly smile, as he moved into the crowd.

The tables were all taken along with most of the space between, so Julian moved back towards a potted palm, standing as close to the wall as was feasible, to get some air. Scanning the room, he saw there were no singles, couples or laddish crowds; everybody was gathered in mixed-sex groups. Eye contact was reserved for the people they knew; strangers didn't stand a chance.

He felt stupid on his own, and tried to spot Gavin. It was possible he'd gone round the corner, so he edged over for a better look. The front line of the bar was visible, but he couldn't see a familiar face amongst the leaning hoards. Michael's face showed up for a second, and then he saw two of them together, standing back from the bar.

When he reached them, they stopped talking, and Gavin passed him a tumbler of something red and icy. 'I've been keeping this warm for you.'

'I didn't know you were here yet,' Julian said to Michael, tasting his drink.

It was the first time he'd bothered with alcohol for three years. He wasn't teetotal, as such, and it wasn't a problem anymore, but he found it easier to stay away from it. When he was thirteen or fourteen, there were times he couldn't get up without a swig of Martini. He was the one to start a cider cult with his mates on the park, wasting the hottest summer of the decade in drowse. It didn't matter at that age, but if he became so enthralled with drink again, it could be distracting. One night wasn't going to make any difference though, so he drank freely, without fretting over the consequences.

His friends were more co-operative now. If the conversation strayed on to people Julian didn't know, or events he'd missed out on, they would explain. Rather than excluding him, they used his unfamiliarity with the stories as an excuse to recount them again. Only once or twice did Gavin lean over to Michael's ear, whispering something that made them both laugh. Each time, Michael would look at the floor until he straightened his face. Julian looked around the room, smiling, hoping they couldn't see his discomfort.

When he looked back, Gavin was pulling a peculiar face, cross-eyed, one eye drifting. Michael did this in response, and they both looked at him sideways, laughing, then did it again.

He couldn't tell if it was a shared joke, or if they were making something out of the fact that he didn't like holding eye contact for more than a few seconds. Was that the face he pulled when talking to people?

Michael put his hand on Gavin's chest, patting, and shook his head, implying that he thought the joke had gone too far. This show of compassion made it even worse for Julian. He told them he was going to the toilet, speaking quietly so they wouldn't hear him. It might make them think.

The urinals were all free, but once that was over, he had to queue for a sink. They were blocked off by mirror-gazers, flicking hair and stroking chins, in the belief that it made a difference. He hoped nobody was looking, when he stared himself in the face, trying to recreate the expression. He couldn't tell whether he went cross-eyed not, when shifting in and out of eye contact. He must have moved closer to the mirror, leaning over the sink, because the next time he exhaled his face was obscured by the fog of his breath.

*

Pia's intercom crackled more than it communicated. Moving back from the doorstep, he looked up at her room, to see that the light had come on at last.

The intercom rumbled. 'Who's there?' her voice said.

He moved closer to the aluminium grill. 'It's Julian.'

She was speaking, but the break-up filtered her words into static.

'I can't hear you,' he said.

'Are you cold?'

'Yes, it's freezing. There's frost on everything. I've walked about two miles. I ran out of money.'

It occurred to him that he must have spent his Unique Coins on the taxi fare, when he gathered his change. A thirty quid prop blown on an extra hundred yards up the hill.

The intercom went quiet, apart from the sound of Pia breathing into it.

'Are you there?' she said. Although indistinct, the speaker was loud, and Julian was grateful the street was empty.

'Yes.'

'Push.'

The door buzzed, and he made it into the fluorescent stairwell, the cold melting from him.

*

While she continued to talk, Julian stared at the old fireplace, now sealed up with cardboard and masking tape, painted over with one coat of gloss. Fibres of the hardboard remained around the edge.

When she stopped chattering, he was too tired to say anything else, unable to recall if she had asked him a question. He heard her put her glass down and saw her walk across to him, then kneel.

She sat between his knees, holding his hands, massaging her fingers over his shining knuckles where his chilblains had erupted. The bone itself appeared to be swollen, and his joints scraped when he flexed them.

She held his wrists, bringing her face in front of his, pushing his legs apart with her hips. Her eyes flicked from one side to the other, trying to find a reference point, to make him return the gaze. Her lips were pushed forward, the moisture inside almost brimming over the edge. If she pouted any more, she would drool.

'Can you feel this?' she said.

Bits of red wine were stuck between her teeth, like crimson fillings. This close, he could see ash coloured wax in her pores, dryness scaling from her cheekbones, and over it all, a clammy suggestion of wetness.

'Can you feel it?' she said, her eyes going liquid.

Sinking back into the chair, he said, 'No, I can't feel anything.'

*

Julian heard a phone ringing in the hallway, then being answered, Pia's voice tired and annoyed. He opened his eyes to morning light, arching the solid curve out of his back, where it had sagged into the chair. At some point, Pia must have covered him with a blanket. It was woollen and itchy, but held in the warmth.

He could hear her say Michael's name, and held his breath to catch what she was saying. There were pauses, mutters, then she said, 'No you can't. I think you should leave him alone.'

His knuckles were split, the slits looking like slithers of gum. He licked with a relaxed tongue, tasting the meatiness of the wounds, leaving saliva to soothe them.

Pia's voice crackled, covered by a fluttering sound. Sitting up, Julian looked at the window. A starling was floating at the glass, its wings smacking down into air. Against the flat brightness of cloud, its struggles left an afterimage, until its wings slowed and ceased. It remained in place, head hanging, beak parted with the surrender of effort.

In the hallway, Pia said something about tomorrow, and put down the phone.

Them Belgiums

Some people say there's beauty in everything, if you know how to look. But they've probably not spent much time in Belgium. I've driven through that country about two hundred times in the past few years, and managed to get through without stopping, not even for a piss. I'd slap the heater on full, and get the van to the ferry as fast as possible, not wanting to pause in such a hideous place. There are no seasons in Belgium, only changes in the severity of rainfall. The clouds let through a chilled, doughy light, which makes it feel like evening all the time. In England the leaves go yellow and glow at the end of the year; it's comforting, a little reward of colour before winter. In Belgium, the pine trees just get blacker the more it rains. They hold water in the air, so the country is swathed in a constant misty drizzle. When I was forced to stop south of Brussels last October, I thought I'd hate every frozen minute of being there. It was a surprise to see two beautiful things in one day.

Normally, I don't drive further than Wiesbaden, just an hour over the German border. There's a warehouse there, where I sell secondhand rock CDs for obscene prices. The Germans have a surprising amount of old jazz vinyl, and they're keen to trade it off, which is convenient. The journey's shorter than you'd think, if you get through Belgium quickly enough.

This time I went four hours further east, to Chemnitz, because I'd heard about an auction where they were virtually giving away van loads of rarities. One Pres Young record alone paid for the petrol. The auction was badly organised, though, and didn't finish until four o'clock. I hadn't accounted for the distance, or Friday traffic, and my eyelids thickened hours before I was due to reach the port. Exhaustion forced me to pull off at Tournelle, north of Spa. It looked more like a village than a town, apart from the massive football stadium, crowded with eight huge floodlight stacks, which illuminated the rain around them.

I knew I would have to find a cheap guesthouse quickly, because I was too tired to drive safely, but I wanted a better look at the stadium. The road ran by the edge of a fenced off carpark, and I could make out signs which showed that the place had been funded by several EC grants. A nearby placard said there was a match tomorrow afternoon. Tournelle vs Bruges. A vandal had spray painted the word 'ballet' across this, in red, which didn't make much sense at the time.

My sleep that night was deep, despite the fact that Mme Barrault insisted the heating be left off throughout the guesthouse. 'We wait until November,' she said in well-rehearsed English, 'For winter.' It wasn't the cold that bothered me, so much as the damp which made the duvet sticky.

My need for sleep pushed me through discomfort, and I slept until after breakfast. I try to avoid sleeping in foreign hotels, because they make me homesick. There aren't many people to miss, but sleeping so far from home means hours and hours without a word to anyone. It makes me tearful, sometimes. Having got through without a frown, I was proud of myself.

The only thing that bothered me was the thought of my City season ticket. We were playing Bolton, and we'd probably slaughter them. I couldn't make it back in time, but it felt wrong to go an afternoon without football.

As I wandered out into the fresh, wet air, I could see the floodlights of the stadium between the trees of the park opposite. I could head straight through for a look, or I could find some food, a baguette, or the Belgian equivalent. I opted for the latter, which turned out to be a glazed loaf, dusted with purple-black poppy seeds. It was dry, but edible, and it gave me enough energy to walk over to the stadium. There was no real reason to go there, because I had no reason to watch their match, except that I might see some goals. I could even cheer on the local side. I wouldn't be missed if I didn't go back today, so there was nothing to stop me from staying.

That wouldn't have been the case three months ago. I tried not to think about Alice while abroad, but she was unavoidable now. We never exactly lived together, but she slept over at my flat so often we may as well have done. She came to one game with me a few weeks after we met, to show interest, which was good of her. Except that she picked her hands all the way through, and never looked up.

'Watch the match,' I kept saying, and she'd glance up, raise her eyebrows, then concentrate on her flaking cuticles. She missed two scorching goals, and I didn't enjoy them the same, because I knew she was bored. I felt silly jumping out of my seat, and she looked at me as though I was stupid.

Alice had no understanding of football, especially when it came to television.

'Look away now,' said Michael Buerke, part way through the news, 'if you don't want to know the scores.'

I covered my eyes, and begged Alice to do the same.

'I'm not covering my eyes,' she said, making a fluffing sound after the last syllable, to show disapproval.

'Please.'

'I've seen them now.'

'Well don't let me know,' I said, certain she'd give it away.

'It's only a game,' she cussed, leaning on to me, her body all sloppy, arms seeming far too long. I sat up trying to breathe more easily, wondering if she could possibly keep a secret until the match was over. That was about two and a half hours from now. Unlikely.

'Stop worrying. You'll enjoy it.'

'Oh, so that means we won.'

She smirked. 'I'm not saying anything, but I can't wait to see your face.'

When the match highlights came on, I spent more time trying to work out her body language, than I did watching the game. Afterwards she went straight to bed, my bed, expecting me to follow.

When I walked in she was curled up, face hidden. She didn't speak for about two minutes as I stripped off, and then as I was about to get in, she said, 'Well your team won, I don't know what you're so bothered about.' And then a minute later, 'I don't know what you're sulking for.'

She was also prone to saying, 'You watch your football,' trying to sound all understanding. Which meant, Don't you dare watch. If you have any interests other than me, you're a shit.

Why do we waste our time with these people? It will never work out. Even if you stay together, she's going to piss you off like this every time there's a game on. Or any time she's not getting exactly her own way. That's no way to spend your life. But we're told to be considerate, to work at it, sort it out, say sorry. There's more to life than football. So you agree, calm things down, apologise.

But then you find yourself sitting in the bath, door locked, muttering, 'What's the fucking point?' to yourself, while she's on your phone to her mates, making plans for the night. At that moment you should stop, because in all honesty you'd rather watch the match than spend more time with her. She says that's not the issue, to shut you up. It's not football. But you can guarantee that if you're going to make her happy, there won't be any talk of goals this afternoon.

Everybody has somebody they regret, my mate Colin used to say to me. It was just a phrase he liked repeating when things weren't going well for me, or when he was especially boxed. It always seemed fitting, and we'd both nod slowly. I regretted everybody I'd been out with, because I never really wanted to be with them.

My face was red, thinking about this, but it cooled as the air was made frosty as I passed into the shadow of the Tournelle stadium. Getting a ticket for the match was no problem, because the population of the town could easily fit into the stadium. Even with a keen following and a strong appearance by the visitors, there were spaces. I had no intention of staying longer than that, and vacated my room, begging permission to leave my van on Mme Barrault's car park. I planned to come straight back and get the late ferry, once the match was over.

*

The teams ran out to polite clapping, until Flensse trotted on to the pitch. He was built like rugby player, but he also looked hollow, because his movements were so light. His skin was unaccountably brown, almost Asian in comparison to his countrymen. His nose was broken in two places, spread across a thick head.

The crowd chanted: 'Ballet, Ballet.' I don't usually like football being compared to art, or dancing, or anything like that. It's just football. The way he moved, though, even when warming up, made me think his nickname didn't lose anything in translation. He was on tip-toes the whole time.

Their crowd didn't throw bog rolls or bits of paper, like we used to, but flowers. Roses, carnations, even bushy chrysanthemums. Red and yellow, like the Tournelle strip. I couldn't imagine our lot chucking flowers. Too girlie for starters, and what's more, you can't nick them from the toilet. The plants didn't have quite the same travel as the soft-strong and long, but the effect was more pleasing.

Flensse never acknowledged the crowd, even though their shouts of praise were quite frantic at times. The closest he came to me was about twenty yards, and I saw him coughing up. He kept the gob in his mouth, concentrating on the ball, and just as I expected him to spit it out, his Adams apple bulged. He swallowed his own gob. There was a tiny, yet audible, sigh from the crowd around me, admiring his restraint.

Tournelle only had one tactic. Pass to Flensse. He would do the rest. He was marked by half the Bruges team, but if the ball came near him, he just walked between them and took it away. His size made you expect him to lumber, but he minced, then moved with alarming sharp strides, and with a chipping movement, plopped it in the net time after time. You could say there was beauty in that, if you looked hard enough, but that might be distorting the truth. It was good to watch, impressive, skilful. The man was an original, but he held his moment of beauty back until the second half.

It was dark by half-time, and the air was becoming foggy. After a few minutes, I couldn't see the other side of the pitch. The floodlights didn't cut through the fog, but swelled in it, making the space in the stadium into a steady, cold flare. When the players emerged, the mist was so thick they could hardly see each other.

In any other country, the match would probably have been called off. In Belgium they had to play on in these conditions, or they'd never get through a game.

The silhouette of Flensse seemed more substantial than the rest, and where the fog slowed them like a syrup, he skipped on. At times, there were only a few players in sight, and I hardly saw the ball. It was probably the same for the players, and no goals were scored. The crowd went quiet, trying to hear where the ball was, listening for the dulled sound of the whistle, and the yelps of pain from secretive fouls.

Towards the end of the game, it rained ferociously, and the fog was flattened away in seconds. The floodlights shone on the soaking grass, and the players resolved into focus. Flensse had the ball, and for a change he passed it across, ran forward, stalled to avoid off-side. Then he began to run with a look of certainty that made me know he was going to score. Bruges saw it too, and ran at him from all sides. From his left, the ball was lobbed clumsily across. It never hit the ground, but strummed of Flensse's right with a snap. It was as though two curved lines had been drawn to that exact point; the curve of the ball, and the arc of his foot. Sacred geometry. Perhaps it was the water and light on the ball, but it appeared to spark as his foot made contact. Everything about the day had led to that moment. The ball sank into the net at the same moment Flensse padded on to the ground, arms by his side, head down as though embarrassed. The others cheered and leapt, and although they danced around him, they knew better than to maul him.

When you see something beautiful, you don't celebrate or scream. You feel lonely. Beauty reminds you how much you are on your own, because there's nobody to share it with.

Afterwards, I felt quite strange and stayed in my seat until most of the crowd had gone. I had no memory of the goalies, because one had nothing to do, and the other could do nothing to stop the ball. It was only five o'clock, but so dark it felt later. I tried to pick out each spot he'd scored from; there were six patches in all, but my gaze kept returning to the place where he landed the last one.

It can only have been ten minutes later that I saw something else. Managing to get lost inside the stadium, I came out of the wrong exit, and walked round the perimeter to get back on track. I looked for a dark place in front of the lights, and guessed it would be the park. The road curved that way, so I followed, walking slowly, enjoying the rain cooling my skull.

On the corner of the main road and the park, I saw the florists where Tournelle must have bought their flowers. It was closing for the night. The girl who worked there was taking flowers inside. She drew a bunch from its green pavement bucket, shook the sappy water off and went inside. She came back, eased the bucket over, its water sloshing into the gutter. She did this four times, as I walked up. Light came from the shop windows, the pavement shining like ice. I could hear every drop, the squeak of stems as she gathered them together, and even from this distance, I saw every movement of her hair, her hands. The fifth time she came out, I saw her face.

When you see a good looking person, what is it that stirs you, even if you've never spoken to them? Even if you stand no chance of ever smiling at them. I didn't realise at the time, but looking back, I think it was the simplicity of what she was doing, emptying water, taking in flowers.

There was nothing to it, but the light and smell and the sound of her hands shaking that water. It made me feel sad for her, but I couldn't tell why. Perhaps it was the dark and cold, or the fact that I wanted to talk to her and knew I probably wouldn't. I slowed down to get a better look. Inside, she put on a duffel coat and a satchel, turned off the light, and came out as I approached. Her hair glowed in the streetlight, and her eyelashes were stuck together with rain, making them look sparkly. She adjusted the straps on her satchel, wiped her face, and smiled.

It's easy to say that I was deluded about all this. A goal is a goal. A pretty person you've never spoken to is just that. But I don't think so. The point is, we both turned up at that moment. I was there by mistake, in the wrong country, a day late, walking back down the wrong road. She was leaving work. Meaningless coincidence, you could say. But I can't get Flensse's goal out of my head. The geometry going on, between his leg, curving and arcing with exact mathematics, to intersect the line of the ball, at that one moment. I'm not sure who's responsible for that sort of precision.

I almost walked past her, but stopped and smiled. It was more like a grin, and I'm surprised she didn't walk away, thinking I was weird.

What did we share? She looked up at the stadium, still not knowing I was English.

'Flensse,' I said. 'Six nil.'

It was only a starting point, I know that. And I was brought there by chance, not effort. But when so many things come together at once, you know that something good will follow. It's the moment of contact that counts.

The Closing Hand

S imon wished there was some traffic on the A82, to distract him from the landscape. Most of the trees had been torn down, their trunks split and shattered amongst those left standing. The leaves were curiously drained and wilted, as though autumn had come a month early.

Storms were forecast, but the sky was featureless white. That was a relief, because he didn't want to put his face-tank on. It only held an hour's worth of air, and the last inhabited village was more than an hour behind. The next one might be as far again. If it came to that, the tank would only put off the suffocation, no matter how fast he drove. There were other cottages in the surrounding hills, but he doubted they would welcome him in an emergency.

Approaching Loch Gar he saw the tip of an acceleration tower, between the Ceann Mountains. The rest of its structure came into view, rising from the loch bed where the water had steamed off. It looked like a studded tube of granite, the anchoring buttresses chalked with mud. The parched ground around it was limy, darkened by cracks like black lightning.

The clouds were becoming thicker. It could be the time of day, he thought, or it could be a storm. His hands were sweating, gripping the steering too tightly, and he wondered if the tower was still active. If so, he was close enough for the magnetics to churn his emotions. That probably wasn't the case though, or the valley would be camped out with travellers. Jenny would be with them, up to her knees in blissful filth, dancing in its vibes.

She had a four day advantage on him, which meant she could be anywhere in Scotland. The main towers were being ignited in the Torridon range, so she would head there. Since leaving Devizes that morning, his aim had been to find her, but now that time was approaching, he wondered what he could say to convince her to come home.

Something flashed in the dark area of sky, then sparked again. The engine misfired twice. He couldn't hear thunder, but knew the storm was coming, and he would have to drive beneath it. If he kept his speed up, the engine should keep firing no matter how much EM fouling the weather caused. The real worry was how much oxygen the storm would steal. It might only last twenty minutes, half an hour at the most, but the winds that came after it would make driving impossible.

The road turned left, going uphill, and if he remembered rightly, the next few miles would be spent heaving the car around slow bends. There were barriers where the drops were severe, but it was still too dangerous to go fast. It would be a struggle to keep the engine revving on the tight corners. More flashes passed through the clouds, and the engine stuttered out for more than a second.

Holding the steering with his knees on the last straight length of road, he strained for the map book and found page 93. It was an old atlas, lots of areas hand-shaded out with pencil to show lost ground, but the road markings were accurate. The map confirmed his suspicion, so he threw it back down, and turned into the first corner, the camber slewing him towards the barrier. The valley was darker than the last, the road arcing in and out of blind corners. It brightened in a steady flicker as the storm built, the engine responding with grumbles.

He could smell magnesium and something like cinnamon, before the rain hit. The first drops on the screen looked like sand, until they spread. Fatter drops followed, slowing the movement of the wipers.

Simon pulled the face-tank on to his knee and primed the valve. He slowed for the next corner, but revved hard again to get through it. The headlights were coating with slime, the beam from them now short; it didn't reach the tarmac or the barrier, and only showed up rain, making it more difficult to see. He refused to slow down, knowing he had to keep the engine active.

The stone banking to his right overflowed with snow coloured water, which smacked against the side window, and as he hit a puddle, the steering went slack.

When the back wing of the car hit the barrier it made more of a thud than a bang, and he braked. The windscreen wipers froze, the screen coating with rain. He didn't feel an impact, but knew he must have hit the barrier again, because his chest creased in pain, and the windscreen flew out like powder. Salty rain covered his hands, stinging.

With the mask on and the valve released he could breathe again, but his ribs felt torn, every breath sharp. He got straight out, and set off downhill, his right hand constantly wiping mucky water from the visor.

For the first time he heard thunder, a sucking roar of sound, followed by booming. There was so much electrical activity, it was impossible to tell which flash matched which sound. There was still some delay, which meant it wasn't overhead yet.

Walking downhill was easier than expected, so he jogged, eventually finding a rhythm that let him run. The road was clear of rocks, the only problem being puddles, which were sometimes deep enough to make him trip. Even though the visor was sticky, it was easier to see than it had been from the car.

The map had shown a property area two miles forward, but there was no way of knowing whether it was inhabited. If the storm passed, it wouldn't matter. Any building still standing in the Highlands could protect him from the coming winds.

It didn't take long for the buildings to come into view; a two storey cottage, and several stone barns, none with lights on. There were no cars or wagons that he could see. The rain had stopped, and the clicking on the valve in his mask meant the air was breathable again. He ripped it off, his attention now moving to the burning in his skin, itching from his scalp, down his neck, around his ankles, but mostly on his hands. The trickling of the water around him was soon replaced by the first shrieks of the wind.

The road levelled out, but he kept up his speed with the aid of the wind. The windows in the ends of the cottage were boarded up, but those in the side were intact. When he reached the front door, it was flung open, and a figure backed away. The wind was too loud to hear anything she said, but it looked as though she was screaming. As she backed off, she stumbled down to her knees.

The wind made it difficult to breathe, so he stepped inside

and leaned against the door to close it, snapping two bolts across. He could hear her voice now, not frightened, but pleading.

'I'm sorry, I'm sorry, I'm sorry,' she repeated.

He didn't know what to say, so looked in to the next room, to see what she might have done wrong. There was nothing there, except two wooden chairs, and a small rucksack.

'I didn't know you were coming back,' she said, her hands open in a rigid claw-like gesture. Her chin was dribbled with spit.

'I don't know who you are,' he said.

She sat back, slumping against the wall.

'Do you live here?' he asked

For the first time she looked as though she understood. 'No. Don't you?'

'No. I was trying to get out of the storm.'

He expected her to smile, realising her mistake, but she put her hands together as though praying, and pressed them against her mouth in jerking movements.

'Do you mind if I shelter here?' he asked.

'There are two rooms upstairs,' she said, eyes still closed, relief entering her voice. Her expression changed then, squinting as though she was struggling to picture something. 'Do you want food?' she asked.

'I haven't brought any.'

'I'll cook.'

She went past him, through the first room, and he heard her swilling tap water, arranging pans. He went upstairs briefly, to wash the worst of the filth from his hands and face, then ached his way back down. Too tired to help or question her, he sat in one of the chairs, moving his attention between her actions and the humming windows. Outside, the wind was fierce enough to lift dirt into the air, scouring the glass.

The soup only took a few minutes to warm from the can. She handed him his bowl, then sat on the floor by the window.

Once she had a mouthful of the food, she asked, 'What's your name then?'

'Simon. I'm heading up to the Torridons. Looking for somebody.'

'Yeah, me too.'

She told him that she was called Rebecca, and that she was trying to catch up with her friends.

'I thought I'd be able to hitch up here, but there's hardly any cars in the afternoons. It's taken me days to get this far. The last driver was an oxygen stinge. He was going to kick me out at the first sign of a storm, but he dropped me here for shelter. I had to jump out while his car was moving. He wouldn't even stop. There was hardly any air down here. I nearly died.'

She finished her soup, despite talking so much.

'I'm going to bed,' he announced, unwilling to go into more detail, too tired to risk a long conversation.

He chose the quietest room. There were no beds, but woolly blankets were piled in the wardrobes, and the floor was carpeted. At first he was comfortable, nested in a corner, and resisted sleep because he enjoyed the lingering tiredness. The floor was too hard though, and the sound of wind soon annoyed him.

The night was a process of turning, waking, moving in and out of exhaustion, too tired to wake up properly but too riddled with energy to sleep. His dreams were never clear enough to be anything other than anxious. Then he dreamed of standing in front of a wide window at sunset, its light shredded on the wet tarmac. It was a windless evening, one star showing above the mountains. The star went out as he watched, and he heard knocking, a door opening. Rebecca was in the room with him.

'Morning,' she said, then frowned, seeing his confusion. 'Are you all right?'

He licked his lips, tasting sugary traces of the rain.

'I thought I was asleep,' he said, touching his ribs. 'I don't know how long I've been awake. I thought it was night again.'

'You must be tired,' she said, and he thought she'd missed the point.

It was still early, but he didn't want to lose time, so explained about his car, and asked if she wanted to come with him. Her rucksack was already packed, leaning against the door. He drank directly from the tap, gulping down more than was comfortable in case he wasn't able to find water again today.

The brightness outside gave everything outlines and shadows. The wind had catalysed the rain, so the grass and heather looked glazed rather than flaky. There was more blue sky than he had seen in a week, but it was unlikely to be stable. Even as they walked, he saw trails of cloud condensing.

When he saw the car, a black hole where the windscreen should be, he looked around for the glass, but it had all been taken by the storm. The car itself hadn't moved, and was lodged against the barrier. The key was in the ignition, and it started first time. He drove tentatively down the hill, but was soon confident that nothing had been damaged. His eyes watered, because of air blasting through the gap. Once they were past the cottages, Rebecca asked who he was looking for.

'Somebody called Jenny. She was my girlfriend. We were living together.'

'She left you?'

'I thought so. She left a note in our flat, said she'd gone. I thought that meant she'd left me. It took me a while to find out that she'd come up here, with most of her friends.'

'She came for the towers?'

'I think so.'

'So you're getting back together then?' He shrugged, so she added: 'You think the vibes will bring you together?'

'No,' he said, about to explain, but Rebecca held up her hand.

'Don't worry. It never fails. She'll love you again.'

'You don't understand,' he said, trying to talk while keeping a safe line up the road, which climbed again, the slope to the left now more like a cliff. 'I want Jenny to come home. I don't want those things to affect her.'

'Your funeral,' Rebecca said. 'But I doubt your friend will want to leave.'

'Because the towers are so addictive?' Simon asked, unable to conceal his anger.

'It's not addiction. The towers are an opportunity. Everybody who goes there finds, something, something so good. It's peace, a togetherness. A something…'

'A something what? You're not making sense. What do they find?'

Rebecca's face dropped. 'It's a togetherness.'

'It's a lot of people getting their brains fried. The towers weren't set up for this. You're being damaged by a side effect.'

'It's not dangerous, Simon,' she said, and he was annoyed at the way she used his name. 'Even the government admits it's not dangerous. Otherwise they'd move us on.'

'They can't admit to the risk.'

She shook her head, her mouth in a cross between a frown and a smile, as though he was too ignorant to understand. 'What can be wrong with everybody coming together, and loving each other? Everybody feeling warmth and joy for each other.'

'The towers are put there to accelerate stability. That's all. To bring an even temperature.'

'That's not what I'm on about. I don't care what the towers are meant to be for. The thing is, they make us good. They give us love. What can be wrong with that?'

'It's empty. It means nothing. You might feel emotions for people on the surface, but it can't be real love. Why should everybody love everybody else? I don't like everybody, and I don't want to. I want to love somebody because they appeal to me, because we can get on, share things.'

'That's so conditional.'

'It makes sense. It would be wrong for me to forget about Jenny. She needs another chance.'

'Typical male thinking. Save the poor woman from herself.'

'It's nothing to do with that.'

'Then let her make her own mind up.'

'That's my point. She doesn't know her own mind, not while she's being poisoned.'

Rebecca paused. 'You really think logic will bring your Jenny back?'

He didn't answer, deciding it best to leave her to it. If she'd been converted by rumours, without even experiencing the buzz, she would never be dissuaded. At least she might help him to find the travellers.

The road meandered through meadow flats, between the tallest mountains so far. He could smell flowers, perhaps the late gorse. Everything was flowering at the wrong time of year. He looked at the fields, seeing only poppies and daisies, and wondered if fatigue was affecting him.

They passed four inactive towers, which crusted out of vanished lakes. Each time, Rebecca moaned disappointment. The only habitation they came across was at the Kyle of Lochalsh, a village of tiny houses, surrounded by rusting cranes, derelict boats and trains. There were no people, and although there was a filling station, the pumps were dry and unresponsive.

Rebecca urged him to drive on. 'Before long you won't care about your precious car. You'll walk everywhere.' Simon wanted to be more practical than that. Finding Jenny wouldn't be enough; he would have to make escape easy, tempting, or it would never become an option. They would need the car and a tank of petrol, but he pressed on, hoping fuel would turn up on the way.

Rebecca's words were prophetic, because the road was soon lined with abandoned vehicles, from motorbikes to cars, wagons and camper vans. Every mile or so there was a new gathering. They were arranged at different angles, left hastily rather than parked.

'We're close. This is the letting go.'

Simon tried to keep his speed up, despite the cluttering. It was possible the travellers had walked to a minor tower in the Glen Carron lochs, he thought. After that, they could have trekked north again, towards Loch Maree. It was due to go active at any time.

It took twenty minutes for their destination to come into sight, and neither of them spoke. The unusually flat stretch of ground between the mountains brought Loch Maree into view when it was eight miles away, a tantalising strip of light with the huge spiked tower rising at other end. The southern coast was lined with trees, largely undamaged by storms, their leaves still green. There were other colours in the trees, and movement.

'We've found them,' Rebecca said, her voice croaky.

The travellers would be weary, bored. If he could get there before the activation, he would stand a chance.

Rebecca giggled when she saw the size of the crowd. There were tens of thousands of people, most wearing only one item of clothing around their waists. All looked thin, and strangely, their skin was pale. They moved in a silly dancing rhythm, turning in circles, wafting their arms. He stopped when the volume of people made it impossible to go further, and few of them laid hands on the car, murmuring.

Rebecca didn't speak to him again, but got out.

'When, when?' she demanded, but danced away so quickly

he didn't hear the answer. She was stripping as she went, her clothes dropping to the floor so quickly, he thought something was affecting his mind. The movement had been almost instantaneous.

The first promise he made to himself was to remain fully clothed. If he could do that, there would be a strand of sense to hold him together.

A woman approached him when he left the car, and put one hand on his arm. She was dressed in flowery panties, nothing else. Her body was young, with small, stiff breasts, but her face was that of a forty year old.

'First time?' she asked.

'I'm looking for a friend,' he said, trying not to stare.

'We're all friends here my love,' she said, with a puzzled, uncertain look. Tugging on his arm, she got him to move with the crowd.

'How does everybody survive? What do you eat?' Simon asked, struggling on the uneven ground.

She let go of his arm. 'It doesn't come to that,' she said, jogging ahead.

There was no path to follow, and people were going through the wood in all places, apparently enjoying the zigzagging walk it forced them to adopt. He could see the lake through the trees. There was a deep, repeating thud in the distance, and a simultaneous sigh from the people around him. Many ran faster, arms outstretched.

He saw white flashes beyond the trees, followed by popping sounds. A blast of icy air sucked through the wood. The leaves of the trees bleached and were pulled from the branches, torn into violent confetti. More flashes followed, replacing the cold with waves of heat.

When he cleared the trees he saw a fat, creamy fog, rolling over the water. The sound from the tower changed to a rumble so huge it felt as though it was coming from inside his heart. Water lifted from the loch in fragments and rushed upwards, clouding and spreading into the upper atmosphere. The loch bed was revealed and it grew lighter, making a sound like tearing paper. The travellers ran towards the tower. Only about a thousand got close enough for the main hit. When they fell to their knees he thought they were praying, but they keeled over and went flat.

The bifurcation shock had a clear, circular perimeter, and the living ran into it. He followed, expecting panic from those left alive, but was appalled to see them dancing, gaily striking rags from the corpses as they came apart. The white meat inside the dead was turning to liquid, which rose up in sparks, chasing the water of the lake.

Simon was reluctant to go any closer. Even though the ignition was over, the tower would continue to buzz. He was about to back off, but smiled, having seen a familiar face. It was Rebecca, now completely naked. Her left side was slack, one breast shrivelled to a brown scab, like a walnut. Her arm was thin and bluish. The energy had missed her legs, and only part of her face was gone.

'I was on the edge,' she said. 'My first time and I just missed.'

'I know you,' he said, trying to remember what she looked like before this. 'Is it you?' he asked, his jaw made cumbersome by the joy he felt at finding her again.

She held him. Her poor arm felt like stone on his back, the muscle gone. She eased away, touched his face, stared into his eyes; her own were drunk-looking, happy.

'Jenny?' he asked.

'Yes,' she said, not looking sure. 'Does it matter?' Although her left arm was virtually hanging off, she started dancing. He watched her, glad to see that she was enjoying herself.

Another woman bumped into her, this one much older, but there was no anger. They both laughed. Then they stared at each other, tilting their heads. 'Mummy?' the older woman asked. The one with the withered arm said, 'I love you,' and they embraced.

He closed his eyes, because there was a strong smell of ammonia and cooked fish. When he opened them again, his mummy had gone. It didn't matter, because a naked man was dancing in front of him, waving his fingers at Simon's face. The man had a thick beard which went up around his ears. His eyes were small, but watery. 'I love you,' he said

'Are you my friend?'

The man stopped dancing, his face serious. 'I love you.'

'Jenny?'

'Yeah,' the man with the beard said.

Simon kissed his shoulder, glad that she was home.

Covering Up

Whenever Shaun asked me to go out, his voice was apprehensive, worried that he was a liability. A lot of the time he was, but I knew it wasn't intentional. He never planned to spoil an evening. He didn't ring me up thinking, I'll embarrass him this time. I'll run off and leave him to walk home alone. We'd been friends for five years, so you'd think he'd get used to the idea that I could put up with his habits. If I was going to abandon him, it would have happened a lot sooner. As it was, I was becoming attached.

On the positive side, Shaun would never hint. If he wanted to spend another evening in town, he stated his desire directly. I could take him or leave him. Some people spend hours talking about what you could do, how long it was since you'd been out, how much they wanted a drink. I let them struggle. If somebody wants something, they should say so. If people want to be abstract, they have to cope with the burden of being misunderstood. Which is why I spent more time with Shaun that year than with anybody else.

Sometimes his requests would come late at night, and he'd be more concerned than ever. 'I'm sorry Neil. I know I shouldn't be ringing at this time. Were you in bed?' Usually, his timing was perfect. There are some nights where nothing holds your interest, and you go to bed certain you've forgotten to do something. Then he rings up and suggests a location, and you realise you'd been waiting for it all night.

His guilty phone calls were difficult, because I had to spend more time reassuring him than usual, but at least the conversation was rapid. Often, he would be silent on the end of the phone, and I'd learnt not to keep asking if he was there, if he was all right. To do so would irritate him, and I knew by now that the quiet was a time when he was thinking. I'd hear him slotting coins into the phone, for silence, and I'd wait until he was ready to speak.

He made me feel shallow a lot of the time, because I always speak without thinking. You can start a sentence, with only the idea, letting the words come together as you speak. It's remarkable that we're capable of that, but I admired Shaun's restraint. Every sentence was complete before he spoke it. This meant there were many pauses. I learnt to use them, after a while. Rather than sitting in embarrassment, I would try to think as deeply as he did.

That's one thing he taught me; deep thinking isn't a particular skill, it's the application of time to a problem. Quick conversations do nothing but repeat the surface details of a subject, with an illusion of depth. If you ponder on something for long enough, an idea reveals its details to you.

His excursions into distraction sometimes began in this way, with deep thought leading to anguish. For months, I tried to ascertain the cause of his upset, but nothing was revealed. When I tried to cheer him with triviality, it brought a rush of depression. For a while I thought it might be caused by an obscure E number in his food, or phosphates in the whiskey. Then I thought it might be particular pubs, certain events that triggered it, something I said, or a way that I acted.

Each time I formed a theory, our next night out would prove me wrong, and I was left looking for another trigger. There was nothing, not even the time of night. The only consistency was that it happened every other time we went out. Or thereabouts.

His reactions didn't bother me as much as he thought. I was only worried if it looked like he was going to get us into trouble. More often than not, that happened when we went round my pubs instead of his. The first few times he took me round the gay pubs, (of which there are more than you would think in Lancaster), he was guilt-ridden, thinking he was making me uncomfortable. I didn't care; just more humans to look at, and I assured him that I felt no guilt dragging him round my pubs. On any given night, we would debate whether to go round one set of pubs or the other, never mixing the two on one night. It was like picking a theme for the evening, which is ridiculous, because neither of was ever on the pull. That would have been tasteless, picking somebody up and leaving your friend to stand there watching. I was sure it would be worse for me, because although I'd seen Shaun with boyfriends, he was always sitting across from them. He never touched, teased or kissed anybody in front of me. I'm sure he thought I would be offended. It wouldn't bother me to see him kissing a man, but it would bother me to be left on my own in a club, if he was getting off with somebody. He never did, because we rarely spoke to anybody else when we were out.

The bad nights would end with me going one way, Shaun storming of on his own. I could try to calm him, follow him down a few streets, into gardens, but that usually wound him up further. If I let him disappear, and went home myself, I'd find out the next day that he was fine. If I tried to stop him, he would end up screaming in a gutter, flinging me off when I went near him. On occasion he would kick at bins, throwing discarded objects. He tried to smash the window at McDonalds once, which was foolhardy, because they were still open, and the glass was too thick, leaving him with sore leg. It's the only time I've seen him calm down during one of those episodes. He sat with me on the bench outside, while the McDonalds staff queued at the window. You'd think they'd never seen a piss-head getting uptight before.

He put his hands against his face, and I thought he was crying, until they came away covered in blood. Things like this are supposed to sober you up, but the adrenaline made me worse, and I panicked. I thought somebody had hit him when I was catching up, or that he'd smashed his head into something. For once, it was Shaun reassuring me. He said it happened all the time, when his mood became extreme; sooner or later something had to give way.

'Sort of like a release,' I said

He shook his head. He was never afraid to disagree. Where other people in conversation will say 'yes, but', or agree, then offer the opposite view as softly as possible, Shaun would say what he meant.

'No, it's not a release. If it was, I'd feel better afterwards.'

To hear him speaking this way, even though I didn't follow what he meant, was unique, because the first symptom of his mood swings was a withdrawal from conversation, which could last until the next day. It began with nodding, where he appeared to be hearing me, without joining in. Then it developed to the state where he was watching me, unhearing. Then, he looked away. These preliminaries would last a few minutes, which was better than seeing a bad mood creeping up over several hours. Until his frustration began, we were able to have a good time. Once it was underway, though, I couldn't get a word out of him. It didn't matter what I said, he wouldn't react. Sometimes, his left eye rolled upwards, not so that the iris disappeared, but enough to make me concerned. By this point, there were only a few seconds left before he would leave. The speed with which he forced his way out, made it look like he was chasing somebody. I sometimes got the feeling that he thought I'd left, and was running after me.

Sitting outside McDonalds, the blood drying on his hands, at least I knew I'd brought him back. Until then I didn't think that was possible, once he was on a roll, and I waited, expecting the anger to come back to him. The blood stopped, and he was eager to go home, but something had changed. Whatever he said about it not being a release, I could tell he felt better for it.

*

Shaun was an inherited friend, somebody I knew in the background, because he was hanging around with my brother. Graham was ten years older than me, which meant that we didn't come into contact much. By the time I was old enough to go out drinking, he'd vanished, following his job around the country. A few years ago, it brought him back to Lancaster, and he made an effort to befriend me. Mind you, he made an effort to befriend everybody. He was never one for small groups, so the few times I went out with him, before he moved down to Ipswich, I was always struggling to get his attention. I don't know how he was capable of making so many friends in such a short time, but whenever he organised something, there were at least ten others tagging along. Shaun was one of them, and he held Graham's attention more than anybody.

I spoke to Shaun, in an attempt to find out what Graham was like. His honesty made me laugh, and I enjoyed talking to him so much, that we soon stopped discussing my brother. Sometimes, I laughed so much when Shaun was telling me something quite plain, he must have thought I was putting it on. It was probably because he made me nervous, and his concentration and intensity made me want to relax; whenever he cracked a joke, an hour's worth of tension was unleashed. I probably got on his nerves.

Just before Graham left, Shaun and I would slope off to the side, talking together, rather than with the group. I'd get home exhausted, but excited, and sit up for half an hour, winding down with night time TV, before attempting sleep.

I'd known he was gay from the beginning, which was fortunate, because it wasn't something you'd be aware of otherwise. Whatever we talked about, whatever observations I made, there was nothing about him that could betray his preferences. If Graham hadn't told me off hand, before I met Shaun, I wouldn't have guessed. On Graham's last night, I sat with Shaun at the back of the room, and I suggested we go out together next week. Just the two of us. Before he agreed, he checked to see whether I knew he was gay.

'Yes, course.'

'Thank God,' he said, looking genuinely relieved.

'And you know that I'm not.'

'Yes, yes.' He paused, smiling at me, and I could see he was deciding whether or not to tell me a joke. He grinned, presumably thinking about the punch line, then attempted it. 'I was reading a men's magazine,' he said. 'And there was this questionnaire about laddish traits. One of the questions said, if you discovered that your best friend was gay, would you: A, accept it because he's your friend; B, tolerate him in a crowd but watch out when your alone; or C, keep your distance. They missed out the obvious one. Shag him.'

I laughed more at his unprecedented enthusiasm than his attempt at a joke, but chipped in an additional punch line. 'Or beat the shit out of him.' His expression dropped for the slightest moment, before he smiled. Now I was relieved. I could easily have offended him or worse, frightened him. Graham told me that Shaun was the most nervous person in the world, with an unnatural fear of violence.

The embarrassment passed, and we made arrangements, but in the taxi home that night, while Graham talked about a sofa he planned to buy, I kept thinking about Shaun's joke. Without realising, he'd called himself my best friend.

*

When he was at his worst, I didn't know what to do with Shaun. There was no way of telling whether a night was going to come apart, until it began. By the time I was getting used to him walking off, he decided to make things worse. Instead of waiting until he was out of the pub, he started while we were still inside. I was doing my best to keep talking, having seen him withdraw, hoping he'd take an interest in me and snap out of it. He put his drink down, and gripping his hair at the front, as though he was going to pull it out, started crying. I urged him toward the door, but he knocked me away. I felt like slapping him, but he cried harder now, pushing his way out, with me following, praying he wouldn't knock anybody over, or lash out at them.

I was outside five seconds after Shaun, but he wasn't there. I saw him disappearing down Orchard Road, sprinting, screaming one long note that must have torn his throat. I wasn't up to running, my belly sloshing with Guinness, but the noise he made would get him arrested or beaten up. At the time, I didn't consider the emotional damage he might be doing to himself, by getting so worked up.

The street was narrow and cobbled, with no lights. I couldn't see whether he'd gone down the alleys, or out the other end, so I kept up my speed. I felt myself getting higher with each step, buoyant for a second, before I fell. I don't remember going down, and the impact was over before I knew what was happening. As the pain softened into my hands, I heard him screaming again, quieter, running out of energy. I needed help now, but he was moving away, leaving me to crawl over to the pavement.

Back on the main street, I looked at my hands, which were skinned and studded with gravel. You wouldn't think there were so many sharp particles on such a small piece of road. There was no blood, but they were glassy with the dew of lymph. Three lads came up to me, asking if I was in trouble. They had little heads and mean faces, the sort of hard bastards I wouldn't usually dare speak to. From what they were saying, they thought I'd been attacked, and wanted some of the action. I'd never met them before, but they wanted to get revenge for me. I assured them I was fine, it was an accident, and that I was looking for somebody. As they left, one of them put his hands on my shoulders. 'Take care mate,' he said. 'Go and see a dentist.' I didn't know that my face had touched the ground, but using a shop window as a mirror, I was able to see what he meant. My front teeth were trimmed with black, where the gum had broken. The grazes on my cheek, chin, forehead and nose were bleeding, and at that point they began to hurt.

It's probably because of such incidents, that Shaun was wary of asking me for help. Once, he rang up after four o'clock in the morning, upset that he was bothering me, but needing to talk. It turned out that he'd wanted to ring me all evening, but thought he might disturb me. I called him a cunt, not because he'd woken me, but because he should have called the moment he was lonely. 'You're always welcome, here. If something's bothering you, come round. What the fuck are we friends for.'

He should have accepted that, but said, 'You say that now, but what happens when this goes on and on, and I never get any better?'

There was nothing I could say. Did he want to me to agree with him and say that I'd soon be sick of him, that he wouldn't be wanted? I didn't answer.

'What happens when you're sick of me, Neil, or when Jessica is sick of me?'

The first part of that I could have handled. With carefully chosen words I could have manoeuvred him away from that way of thinking, but it wasn't fair for him to bring Jess into it. She was being more tolerant of him than most people would be, and he should be glad of that. Accusing her of coming between us sounded like a deliberate ploy, something to unbalance me.

'Look, you're welcome, any time. And that's the end of it.'

It didn't sound convincing to me, and when he put the phone down on me, I regretted it. If anybody spoke to me like that when I was in need, I'd never go near them again.

I left a note for Jess – Shaun's in trouble – and went after him. By the time I made it over there, running less than half of the distance because I'm not that fit, he was still outside the phone box, walking up and down. His front door – between two shoe shops – was only a few yards away, but he appeared to be lost. It was mid-December, and he was wearing a vest. This looked strange on him, because even in good weather, he wore shirts and jumpers. Since September, I'd never seen him in anything other than thick clothes, rarely taking his coat off.

He recognised me, and neither of us knew how to react. Should I smile, ask him how he felt, get mad? I hadn't a clue. If this was summer, the sky might be getting light and it would feel early. In winter, half past four just feels late.

'Aren't you cold?'

'I'm having trouble breathing.'

He wasn't keen on going back inside, but I told him that his room would have plenty of oxygen and tried to lead him towards the door.

'And if I start freaking out, if I collapse. What are you going to do then?'

'I'm going to call a doctor.'

I was pissed off with him challenging me. I felt like telling him to accept that I was going to look after him, whatever. He didn't need to keep testing me, pushing me away, to see how much I would stand. It's as though the fear of me leaving him was so great, he could only gain reassurance from seeing me put up with his worst moods. I consoled myself with the thought that he always recovered, but it wasn't much comfort. His recoveries were taking longer, and his depression was more frequent. For the first time, I wondered if he had a point. What would I do if he lost it completely? If there was no pleasure to be gained from being with him, nothing other than reminder of how everything had gone wrong, would I bother to see him? My breathing was as laboured as his, by the time I put him to bed.

The cold must have worn him out, because he slept without talking, and I classed that as a successful conclusion.

Walking home took longer than usual, because the floor was slippery, and I was tired. No sound is quite so narcotic as the whine and clink of a milk float. The more courageous were emerging from their houses by the time I made it back, car engines sounding restrained and muffled. Jessica was up earlier than usual, dressed for work hours before she needed to be, sitting at the table with an elaborate breakfast. She'd been up about ten minutes and looked immaculate, short hair lapping round her cheeks, black polo-neck shirt ironed on to her body. I felt scruffy in her presence, and put the water on for a bath. When I explained about Shaun, she suggested that we take him out. The three of us together, she said, might be able to bring some cheer into his life. It was Christmas after all, and we shouldn't be staying in. I was pleased with this, because she could easily have been jealous. She could have huffed about the way I went after him, or sneered at the disruption, but she was being considerate.

*

Contacting Shaun was difficult, because he refused to install a phone. He said the landlord wouldn't like it, and he would use it too often. When I said that it would be easier for us to reach him, or for him to get help when needed, he looked glum, and said he preferred the freedom of using phone boxes. It seems to be an affliction of the lonely, to isolate themselves.

There's always an element of choice in loneliness. Unless you're camping out in the mountains, you can always make contact with people. You might have to volunteer to work in a soup kitchen, take part in a boring sport, or risk talking to strangers in a pub, but there is always a way to make contact. This doesn't mean loneliness isn't real, but it's misunderstood.

Loneliness is nothing to do with a lack of people. Some of the loneliest people are surrounded by hordes who consider themselves to be friends. The cause of loneliness is dissatisfaction with the company on offer. It's not arrogance, just the honesty to admit that spending time with these people will leave you emotionally famished. You want intimacy so passionately, that you consider friendship something hollow and false. The worst loneliness comes when there's no nostalgia and no hope, only the present moment, with nobody to get upset about.

If this sounds unsympathetic, it's because I've been there myself. Loneliness contains a central contradiction. You want to be rescued by a perfect person, somebody who can cure you of pain, but you don't really believe it's possible. You know you don't deserve to be rescued. You're such a miserable fuck, that if such a person came trotting into your life, you'd be whining her out of the door before you got to know her.

This is why people meet the right person when they give up. There's a semi-mystical belief that when you stop trying to obtain something, it comes to you of its own accord. The idea is that if you wish for something, the act of wishing is confirmation that you don't believe it's possible. Only when you stop wishing, is something allowed to happen. This takes trust, but I've seen it happen to people all my life. While you care, while you really want to find somebody worthwhile and meaningful, you're left clinging to the fattest and ugliest humans, the ones who call themselves 'creative' but haven't got an original thought in their heads. When you finally say enough, no more of that shit, and declare celibacy, something happens. If you really mean it, somebody worthwhile moves into your life. There's nothing paranormal about this; it's just that when you give up, and start making friends, and acting like a human being, you're a damn sight more attractive.

Telling this to Shaun, I was surprised to see him redden, and speak without thinking.

'You're talking shit, you smug bastard.'

That was a week before the phone box incident, and I think he'd forgiven me by then. I didn't have time to check up on him, or ask him out for the meal, so Jess went round during her lunch break. According to her description, he was as well as he'd ever been, more keen than usual to go out.

There are some people who will moan for the sake of it. If you invite them out for a meal, they'll say, 'Oh, I'll have to draw some money out then,' rather than, 'Thanks'. Some of his friends thought Shaun was like this, but that was to misunderstand the man. In some ways, he was the most positive person I knew. He tried to see the good in everything, but he wasn't able to filter his perception the way some people can. He wouldn't use the positive side of something to blot out the negative. If you watched the news with him, he took it all to heart, feeling for every single person that suffered, shouting abuse as the one's who caused it. I'd never patronise him to the extent of telling him to calm down, but I couldn't get as involved. When they showed the funny bit at the end, about an animal or a spaceship, I'd let it cheer me up. That's what it was there for. But Shaun was too tangled up with what had gone before, to forget it. Hours later, when I was too drunk to remember that we'd watched the news, he'd repeat some detail that had bothered him.

The sort of passion kept him occupied, but I don't think the anger did him any good. It wasn't the cause of his depression, but it must have been linked in. Somebody who feels so intensely, is open to abuse.

Late back from work, I rushed to get ready. My best effort left me looking three shades scruffier than Jess. We were only going to Pizza Margarita, so she wasn't dressed up, but on her, black trousers and a polo neck shirt looked fantastic. It was nothing to do with her clothes, but her bones. While I looked as though my frame had been rammed together in a hurry, she was crafted. I've met women like this before, and it isn't always attractive. They're so neat and careful, they refuse to allow character into their movements, their clothes being more like bondage equipment. It wasn't like that with Jess, because there was nothing false or restrained about her.

When we met Shaun, she put her arm round him and drew him out of the house. She looked like the type to go in for air kissing, but wouldn't lower herself to that. He smiled to himself, looking at me sideways for confirmation that her contact was acceptable.

At the restaurant, Jess took hold of Shaun's coat at the shoulders, and he complied, letting her take it from him. If I'd tried such a thing, he would have convinced me that he was cold, and I'd have been happy to sit with him like that all night, no matter how many people stared.

With the three of us were together, it made me realise how rare such gatherings were these days. I saw both of them as much as ever, but it was weeks since we were all out at once. Months, even. We could spend our time talking about those months, what we'd been doing, catching up, which might distract Shaun from misery. The food was ordered, our waitress brought a bottle of red, and Jess asked Shaun what he was up to these days.

He looked at me again, the way children do to their parents, when asked questions by a stranger. He might have thought it was a phoney question, because he knew I would keep Jess informed. He flattened his napkin over his knees, considering his answer. I was growing tense, as he thought about it, but Jess was relaxed, not even reaching for her wine. She looked at him until he answered.

'I'm tired all the time,' he said.

'Is there something wrong with you?' She asked it seriously, then smiled when he looked at her, and he tried to smile back.

I could see what she was trying to do; let him talk about the things that bothered him, without it having to be too gloomy.

'I'm not sure,' he said. 'I've been tired for three years.'

I laughed out loud at this point, and they both looked hurt, so I said it was the way he said it, I knew what he meant, and fumbled my way into deeper embarrassment, ending by saying, 'Well go on, what do you mean.'

Before he could answer, Jess asked him if he was sleeping well.

'Too well. Sleeping all the time, waking up tired, half asleep all day. I never wake up fully. It takes a conscious effort not to yawn. All the time, I'm fighting to stay awake.'

Already the evening was turning into a therapy session, and I resented that. It wasn't that I thought we should be shallow, but I wanted to cheer him up. I doubted that working through his problems was going to make any of us feel better. I'm sure he'd have gone home happier, if we'd had a good time. If I'd said that out loud, though, I'd have been called heartless. Watching her tempt him into revelations, I resented her skill. If he wanted to talk, why didn't he talk to me?

Jess suggested that he try relaxation classes.

'I've already tried that,' he said. The way he looked at me, you'd think he'd said, 'I've been to a peep show.' I was surprised that he hadn't told me, but why he thought I'd mind him relaxing was beyond me. The more she got out of him, the more I realised he was holding things back from me, and I was angry with both of them.

Shaun lightened the mood by telling us about his relaxation therapy. The room they used was an aerobics gym, so it stank of perfume and farts. The only other men looked so weedy and stressed out, he felt worse than he had before he went. The relaxation was brought on by concentrating on different parts of the body, relaxing the muscle groups in sequence, imagining warmth into the joints.

'Did it work?' I asked.

'No.' The smile went out of his voice. 'It didn't work, because everything hurts. If you guide your attention around your body, all you find is pain. You're supposed to imagine healing light, and heat, but the more I thought about my muscles, the more they ached. My knees creaked, my lungs felt tight, I was struggling to breathe. No matter how I positioned myself, my spine felt disabled. It was impossible to relax. Since then, I've found it difficult to sleep. It made me aware of how uncomfortable I am.'

I could tell that Jess wanted to look at me, wondering how we could bring him out of this. She raised her glass and said, 'Thank God for anaesthetic.'

'It doesn't work like that for me,' Shaun said, but he emptied his glass anyway.

Jessica put her hand on his arm and squeezed, getting no response.

Sometime during the meal, I must have stopped listening to them, but then I heard Shaun say something about being gay. Shamefully, I was the only person to look up from my meal. The other diners didn't hear or didn't care. I tried to redirect my attention behind him, pretending that something else had caught my attention. It was rare to hear him say it out loud, to anyone.

I don't know what he was telling he, but Jess responded with a speech.

'What are you spending so much time with Neil for? You should be down the gay bars, pulling men, having a good time. While you waste your time with him, you're doing yourself down.'

He enjoyed her joke, and said, 'You're quite right. He's dragging me down.' We all laughed at that, relieved, I think, that he was enjoying himself, but then he added, 'So long as you don't mind me spending time with him.'

'Shaun. Don't be silly,' Jess said.

Earnest pizza eating followed, and mine was finished. The talkative ones still had most of theirs left, so I went on the scrounge, to keep myself occupied.

'When are you boys going for your Christmas walk?'

'Soon,' I said, even though we hadn't made arrangements. 'That should do us some good, eh Shaun?'

He paused for too long, swallowing his food, then said, 'Yes.'

*

We'd known each other for six months by the time we discovered a shared interest in mountain climbing. Living so close to the Lakes, it was shameful that we didn't go more often, and by teaming up we cured ourselves of complacency. Since my mid-twenties, I'd been climbing less than once a year, but Shaun and myself managed to make it up there once a month, sometimes collecting several peaks in a day.

When I was still at school, my Dad used to let me go to the Lakes on my own. A fourteen year old boy camping by himself isn't something that could happen today. I climbed mountains fanatically, glad to be alone, but spent the nights wretched in my tent, wanting somebody to talk to. I chose rugged, slate peaks such as the Old Man of Coniston, and for a long time I thought all mountains were mined and scattered with broken stone.

The first time I climbed the Old Man, the sun was overhead when I reached the summit. Half way down, I could see a cradled tarn as blue as a swimming pool. I ran out of water on the way, and drank from it. I know now that it's copper sulphate solution, drawn out of the mines by rain, but on that first walk, it looked like a magic lake. I climbed the Old Man six times in that decade, trying to find the same conditions; high sun, blue water, but it never happened. The water remained the same grey as the rock around it. I should have been pleased with the memory, and left it at that. Instead of trying to recreate the past, I could have gone on new walks, made new memories.

With Shaun, walking was more enjoyable, because when I saw something beautiful I could point, he'd look, and by sharing the moment, it was made precious. Shaun was at his best in the mountains. He continued to talk his way through every subject that bothered him, but he never became miserable. If we were soaked, or burned, or aching to the point of feeling sick, we only felt pleasure. Christmas walks were the best, because we chose the worst mountains, and the conditions were always crap. We knew there'd be no view, no time to rest, in cold so severe it could bring on nausea. Whatever else, it was bound to be exciting. Neither of us could remember why we went on the first one, but it became a tradition that we didn't miss.

*

As our plates were cleared away, I knew that if Jess hadn't brought the subject up, we probably wouldn't have gone on a walk that year. My stomach was full of dough, making me reluctant to discuss it further, so I asked for the bill.

We walked Shaun back to his flat, then drove home. When we got into bed, Jessica said, 'You've been quiet ever since I mentioned that Christmas walk.'

'I've been quiet all night. Couldn't get a word in edgeways.' My intention had been to laugh her observation off, but I sounded annoyed. I wanted to take the words back, rephrase them, change the intonation, but it was too late, an argument was born.

'You were sulking, Christ you have a go at Shaun, but at least he can hold a conversation, you just sat there and sulked; it was embarrassing.'

'Embarrassing? You were the embarrassing one, forcing him to talk like that.'

'He wanted to talk.'

'Bollocks.'

'Then why did he?'

'Because you forced him to.'

'Shite.'

'You know I'm right, what's wrong with you, you're acting weird these days?'

'You're the one being weird. Listen to yourself.'

'No, you listen to yourself. Is your period due?'

It went on like that until we realised that we agreed with each other, and were arguing for the sake of it. Only when I'd denied that there was anything bothering me ten times, did I put my finger on the irritation. The thought of a Christmas walk was getting on my nerves. If Shaun had a phone, I could ring him up, make this year's arrangement, and that would be it. I'd be able to sleep.

We hadn't been walking since last Christmas, because we were both ashamed of our laziness on that day. Hung over and cold we set off an hour later than usual, and to catch up, we skipped the usual service station breakfast. With the routine broken, our enthusiasm dwindled. We sat in the car, parked beneath Causey Pike, playing Twenty Questions, getting out to stretch and test the wind, going for a pee. We ate our lunch, followed by the emergency rations, and by then it was too late for a full walk. We managed a hike around the Pike, without reaching the summit of anything, then spent the rest of the night drinking in Ambleside. I lied to Jess, inventing a story about a difficult climb, with winds that knocked us over. My story was told with such enthusiasm, she believed me, and I felt even worse.

How is it that something which is meant to be a treat, becomes an obligation? I think the reason we felt so guilty about that day, was because we enjoyed ourselves more when we stayed in the car, than when we went climbing. We've rarely laughed so much, and I don't think we liked to admit that. It was a sign of our age, that we were willing to talk our way through the day, when we should have been walking.

Jessica was mumbling her way into sleep, but I couldn't get there myself. I was cold all over, but when I went close to her, it was too hot to breathe.

The pizza melted away at last, and I managed to get a few hours.

On the way to work, I dropped a note off at Shaun's, saying that we must go walking. 'And this time walk,' it said.

*

Every so often, Shaun indicated that he might fancy me, which was understandable. I'm not the most appealing man in the world, but there was always the chance he would want something like that, because we got on together. If you're friends with somebody, if you like being with them, you get to like the sight and sound of them. Friendship is a feeling, that makes you want to hold someone.

I know this is true, because it happened with Jessica. We became friends by default, when she turned me down at a party. She didn't want anything like that, but she found me interesting, so we met as friends. I asked her out again a couple of weeks later, and she said we would have to stop being friends if I kept that up. So I changed my mind, saw her as good company, an alternative to Shaun, and forgot about my desire.

We never mentioned the fact that I used to like her in that way. I made a big play of pointing out women that I fancied, and she did the same with men. Before long, we were spending so much time together that all our associates and relatives thought something was going on. No, no, we said, nothing like that. We're friends. We don't even consider it. Which was a lie.

If you possess testicles, it's going to be on your mind. There's a million years of instinct grumbling away inside you. Mix that in with a bit of compassion, and a pleasant afternoon on the beach, and you find yourself harbouring thoughts of love.

To my relief, the same was true for Jessica, even though she was better at denying it. I imagined that one day, we would finally get drunk, and she'd take me in her arms, and that would be it. The friendship wouldn't be destroyed, it would develop into the relationship it was always meant to be.

I was wrong. We kissed once in a night club, following her cousin's birthday party. Some of her friends were there, along with one or two relatives. It was only a kiss, but I think we went at it like maniacs. Once they saw what was going on, Jess changed her mind. I've never heard the word 'friend' so many times in one night, but even as she shouted the explanations into my ear, she kept kissing it. By that point, my willpower was destroyed, and I thought fuck to friendship. I told her I loved her.

Our next few meetings were extremely tense, and it took a long time for me to convince her that I could be trusted. I was banned from her flat, and told we could only meet on neutral ground. We went to see The Baby of Macon at the Dukes, which was harrowing. The audience was smaller than usual, which for the Dukes meant it was down to twenty. Half of those walked out after five minutes of the rape scene. By the end we were both a bit down, and we stopped in the bar for a quick pint; that gave me the courage to put my arm around her as we walked. Then we were leaning against the side of the church, the footpath so narrow we were almost standing in the main road, with Jessica holding my face as she kissed. I nearly fainted on the exhaust fumes.

After that, it was pointless pretending that we didn't want to touch. She was all I thought about, as Shaun would testify. He went through five boyfriends in two months, when I started sleeping with Jessica. I can't blame him; I was never around.

Jessica never asked me to live with her, but I moved in, bits at a time. Having spent a month there, moving most of my clothes, all of my CDs, and my best lamps and candles, I asked if we were going out with each other now. I asked, because I was hoping to get rid of my flat. I could give her half of the rent. She couldn't argue with that.

Unfortunately, she was still convinced that we were friends.

'What's the difference between lovers, and friends who touch?' I asked. I couldn't see any difference. If you like somebody and want to touch them, what's wrong with that? If you want to be with them, then it doesn't matter what you call it.

Jessica explained that it was all to do with commitment and exclusivity. Which must have meant that she didn't want to be committed, or to touch me exclusively.

'So you wouldn't mind if I went off with another girl?'

'I don't own you,' she said, but she wasn't too chuffed. 'And you don't own me,' she added.

There was no point in denying it; I'd be livid if she touched anybody else, even though we were just friends.

We spent that night together, and everything we did was the same as I'd do with a girlfriend. We slept together, kissed each other, she told me that she loved me. I think she meant it. She brought me supper in bed, and called me silly names. The only difference was that she wouldn't admit we were going out with each other.

When I saw that she was enjoying being with me, I gambled, telling her that being friends who touched wasn't on. We either had to go out with each other, or be ordinary friends. If the gamble failed, I knew I could build back up to contact over time, so I wasn't too worried. She wasn't going to kick me out.

'You're trying to trap me,' she said.

It took an accident to make her see sense, which, from what people tell me, is a fairly common experience. I was talking to her about a motor race from the previous afternoon. She appeared to be listening, I was getting excited with the story, and as we reached the church where we kissed that time, I stumbled off the curb. This happens to me all the time, because I walk the curb like a tightrope, but this time, a bus was passing. Its wing mirror clipped the top of my head.

As she nursed me back to health over the next few days, Jessica decide that she couldn't bear to see me hurt. She didn't want to lose me.

'So we're going out with each other then?'

She said yes.

'Thank fuck for that,' Shaun said, when I told him. 'Perhaps we can be friends again now.'

I knew he was kidding, but I admit that we did see more of each other in the following weeks. It was after I moved in with Jessica that he gave indications that he fancied me. Prior to that there had been one or two comments, but I took them as jokes. Now that he knew I was safely wrapped up with a girl, he risked making it more obvious, commenting on my looks, saying he thought I was a good person. Saying things like, 'You're more than a friend could ever be.' My reaction was to laugh at him, because I didn't know what else to do.

*

Time ran out in the last few days before Christmas, so our walk had to be on Christmas Eve. It was either that, or Boxing Day, which would mean sharing the Lakes with hoards of sea-level visitors who wander round the towns dressed for an expedition, never getting further than the cake shop. The mountains would be empty, but we'd resent the traffic.

On the down side, cosmic law dictates that, while Boxing Day is sunny and fresh, Christmas Eve is a winter day. In many ways, I prefer that. It's more in keeping with the maudlin Christmas spirit. It doesn't always rain, but there is a wonderfully tired cold, a hazy wet freeze that makes you seek out the comfort of a country pub. To achieve the best Christmas atmosphere, it helps if the locals are celebrating and cheery, but you're missing somebody special.

Jess was going to visit her cousins in Sedbergh, so I invited Shaun over. We could have a bit of a drink, watch some Christmas TV, pack our butties for the next day, and get an early night. I didn't want to be on my own, and this was a good way of making sure he didn't get into trouble.

We didn't talk much, except to comment on the programmes, which all seemed overtly poignant. We polished off the Glenfiddich, then the Castle Eden, filling up on those cheap pissy beers that come in gulp sized bottles. Shaun went to sleep on the floor, his neck pressed against the base of the armchair. His shirt buttons were undone half way up his stomach, which was remarkably hairless. If it has been a mass of bushy fluff, I'd have looked away and gone to bed, but seeing all that clean skin made me watch him. His stomach rising, falling, shirt gap getting wider.

I'm not gay. I've told Shaun this many times. I can admire the male physique, and I can recognise when a man is attractive, but it doesn't do anything for me. Dicks are interesting to look at, but they don't turn me on. So what was I doing watching my best friend lying on the floor? I didn't get a hard on, though. It wasn't sexual, I'm assured myself, it was just an interest in him, as a physical creature.

He made mewing sounds, cuddling closer to himself. Inside his shoes, I could see his toes curling. I considered getting him a blanket, but he was fast asleep. Better to leave him to it.

I couldn't sleep, knowing that Jessica would be home in an hour or so. I lay in bed thinking about Shaun. There was a time two weeks previously, when I'd come out of the bogs in the Jolly Farmer, to find Shaun being chatted up by this bloke who was twice his age. He wasn't getting anywhere, and Shaun made sure he looked pleased to see me. Once this old bloke pissed off, Shaun said, 'I was going to put my arm around you, so he'd get the message.'

When he said that, I quivered, because the thought of doing something different excited me. It wasn't that I wanted to be like that, with Shaun, but the idea excited me. I didn't get much chance to think about it, because Shaun sank into an anxious mood. It wasn't one of his celebrated froth jobs, there was no disappearing act, but he was close to tears as we talked.

Picturing the memory almost put me to sleep, and when Jessica came in, trying to be quiet, I jumped. Without getting herself a glass of water, or brushing her teeth, she undressed and got into bed. I pretended to be asleep.

*

The roads were empty, so we went up the A6 instead of the motorway, feasting on carbohydrates, drinking enough Lucozade to bring us back to life. We couldn't wake up completely, because it was still night outside. We would need every hour of light, to fit in a decent walk.

Beyond Wythburn, the road is banked on either side, the hills covered with trees. There's no lighting, which makes it one of the darkest places you can drive through. I've been there at night before, and it has always made me uneasy. I wanted to get through quickly, but it's too dark for fast driving to be safe. The rivers coming off Helvellyn leak over the surface, keeping it wet. The road is a series of curves, making it feel as though you are going to slide off. All you can see is ten feet of tarmac in front of you, the glint of a crash barrier, and hundreds of rabbit bodies, some so fresh the meat is bleeding.

Shaun must have sensed my tension, because he said he didn't like the area. There was no other traffic until that point, and then I saw something that looked like an accident. I slowed down, checking behind to make sure it was safe, then crawled towards the light. Two lorries were parked at a slant on the verge, their headlights on full. A car was facing us, its headlights crossing the road, making it difficult to see what was going on. People were moving between the vehicles, some standing with hands on hips, others turning away. When we were alongside, I was able to see what they were looking at. In the ditched gutter a large stag deer was on its back, a crush wound on the side of its face. It was trying to run, legs galloping against the air, its neck unable to lift its head.

'It must have been dead,' I said. 'That was a nerve reaction.'

'I saw its eyes,' Shaun said, and I knew he was right. The deer didn't look frightened, but confused, wondering why it wasn't able to run away. Its antlers were intact, and I tried to picture how the head could have been split so badly, without damaging them.

We pulled into the next parking area, and I said that by the time we'd got our boots on, it would be coming light. The climb up Helvellyn would take five hours at most, up and down, which would mean we'd be back while it was light.

The first half hour was spent getting out of the tree line. The whole of the mountain was obscured, one giant cloud slammed over the whole area. It wasn't raining, but by walking through such wet air, we were dripping in minutes.

For a long time all I could hear was the scrape of my waterproof against my ears, amplifying my breathing. It was too cold for us to rest, and the only stops we made were for food and water. My hands were so numb, I couldn't get the cap back on the water bottle. Shaun tried to put it back, but we could only get it to go back on when I held the bottle in place, and he lowered the cap on with the heels of his hands, nudging it tighter. I could imagine a scenario where we'd need to tie a rope to something, to save ourselves, and our hands wouldn't even be able to hold it.

There was no snow, but it was the coldest I had been. We reached level ground, somewhere near the summit, after four hours. Next to the path, the ground dropped away, and cloud rushed up through the space. I couldn't see more than a few feet down the ridge, but this was clearly a cliff, the wind blasting mist up at us. We leaned against the wind, skin chapping, but enjoying the force. It felt like we were skydivers, flying down the side of the mountain, dizzy with the speed.

I'd been thinking about turning back since we left the tree-line, but didn't want to be the first to suggest it. The sky was getting darker, which meant the cloud was thickening, or it was later than we thought. My watch was concealed beneath elasticated cuffs, and my fingers didn't have the strength to pull them back to check. Shaun was slapping his arms against his body, neither of us moving further up the path, but not daring to suggest we give up.

'Do you think it's getting dangerous?' I shouted over the wind. I couldn't believe how feeble my voice was against the storm. Shaun nodded. 'Should we turn back?'

When he nodded I set off down hill, puzzled by how tired I felt. When I saw news reports about people dying from cold, giving up and dropping into the snow, I could never understand it. If your life's at stake, that fear would wake you from anything. After stumbling a few times, I knew that if I fell, that would be it, I'd be sound asleep. The desire to sit down and rest, to close my eyes for just a few seconds was intense, but I kept telling myself that I'd be dead if that happened. And I promised myself that next time I was in bed, unable to sleep because my feet were cold, I'd think about this.

Shaun kept up, but I didn't look back as often as I should. If he'd tripped, I wouldn't have heard a thing, and I might not have had the energy to go back up for him.

I didn't want to be rescued, because every time we'd been walking, a good percentage of our conversation was spent slagging off unprepared walkers who got themselves into trouble. In this case, we'd done everything right, but overestimated our fitness.

And then we were into the trees, back at the car, heating up at an alarming rate. Our hands couldn't cope with zips or buttons, but we both wanted to strip down. The shelter gave our bodies a chance to react to the exposure, the heat making me feel worse than the cold.

When we were down to underwear, I managed to get a towel out of my bag, and scrubbed at my skin. I passed it to Shaun, and was about to apologising for getting it wet before letting him have a go, but he thought I was asking for help, and started drying me with it. I leaned over the steering wheel, letting him get the worst off my back, then he dried my chest and arms.

'Use it yourself,' I said, and looked out of the side window, hoping he wouldn't ask me to return the favour.

*

I've known people who regard depression as an achievement, something to be cultivated, to reveal the complexity of their personality. I've been to parties where the delicate cutters gathered in a corner to share their wounds. One girl waved a pen knife, telling us how much she wanted to have a stab at her hands, waiting until she had a good audience before making the first mark. It was an all-nighter, and by morning she'd cut the quick from her nails, decorating her veins with nicks. Soft-spoken boys were proud of the cuts on their arms, all giving me sad eyes as they told of the pleasure it gave them. There's no pain, they said.

I felt like telling them to keep it to themselves. It's not that I'm unsympathetic, because I'm sure there are some people who do this because they have no other way to cope. But the people I knew were following a fashion. Once they'd pierced their noses, and shaved their heads, what was left but a bit of arm slicing? It looked like self-abuse, but it was safe. If it was something they did in secret, because they were genuinely hurting, and didn't know how else to cope, I wouldn't take the piss. But every single time we went out, the cuts were on show.

If they wanted to hurt themselves, they should have done it properly. The last time I went out with that lot, I lost patience and offered to beat one of them up. If he wanted to be hurt, I'd do it for him. Knock his pansy teeth out.

Steady on, Neil, steady on.

It wound me up, because for all their mock suffering, I knew there were people in real pain. Shaun was the most desolate person I've met, and he never once harmed himself on purpose. And his moods were always real. He would never tense up for the sake of something to do. If he reacted badly, I knew it was because he was in agony.

This was very much on my mind on Christmas Eve, as I sat in the kitchen on my own, in my wet underwear, scratching the skin from my knuckles with a Fosters Ice bottle top.

It's peculiar how trivial things can seem important, when you're in that sort of mood. I got it into my head that, although it didn't matter how much blood got on the table, I didn't want there to be fingerprints in it. I wanted the drops to be neat edged. When I saw my fingertips drying into the blood, I tipped more over it, covering up the lines.

This wouldn't have happened if I wasn't pissed. It's just not in my nature. I won't side-step the issue, by saying I didn't know what I was doing, but if I hadn't been drinking, I wouldn't have sat there pondering like that. And I wouldn't have had the bottle top. I wasn't completely convinced by this line of thinking, so cleared up the bottles and glasses. The cold water I used to clean them with made my hands sting, and brought out new blood.

Five minutes earlier, I wouldn't have cared if Jessica had walked in with her whole family, so long as the were no finger-prints spoiling the even spread of the blood. Now, I was seeing sense, and wanted it all wiped away. I tried cleaning up without seeing to my hand, but gripping the cloth made the wounds wider, leaving more mess. First things first. There were no ban-dages, so I put plasters on. We had plenty of those; Jessica was a collector. I used all the *Lion King* plasters, and some of the plain pink ones, disappointed at how quickly they became damp and loose.

When I heard Jessica at the front door, I smiled at the timing; I'd just rinsed out the cloth for the last time, and had done a pretty good job of clearing up after myself, concocting a story about a fall while we were in the Lakes. She came into the kitchen, and before she even saw me, I knew that I'd fucked up. She put the main light on, making me realise that I'd been clean-ing in a few cheams of light from the lamps, missing most of the stains. When I saw her face, I guessed at what she was seeing; me in my underwear, sodden plasters coming away from my savaged hand, and streaks of blood wiped into the grain of the table.

My story worked. Either she didn't want to know this was happening to me – not on Christmas Eve for God's sake – or she was too tired to think. I went into so much detail, she must have realised I was lying. She didn't even want to see my hand.

'Are we going to do anything Christmassy then?' I asked.

'Let's just go to sleep.'

Watching Over Me

Before the campsite expanded to take up all of my Dad's land, there used to be an orchard. Unable to sleep my Dad would start work as soon as there was enough light to see by. He didn't have much enthusiasm for the toilet block or the shop until January, so he spent autumn in the orchard, putting new stones on the paths, strengthening the fence, and clearing the leaves. When he lit a fire to burn them, I could hear the crackling from my bedroom.

He knew I liked fires, but never told me when they were planned. Dressing as quickly as I could, I ran down the land and joined him. He laughed at the sight of me. 'I thought you'd be out if I lit this,' he said, piling more mulch on to the smoulder. 'Let me show you something.' He always seemed anxious when talking to me, unless he was explaining. That morning, he held up a leaf and told me why it changed colour.

'The yellow is always in there, but it's hidden by the green. In winter, the tree doesn't need green, so it's taken away, and you can see the yellow. I don't pretend to understand.' It was a phrase he used all the time when explaining.

'What about red leaves?' I asked.

My father looked up.

'We get more of them when it goes cold quickly. The tree puts cork on the end of the leaf and bottles it up. The sugar that's trapped inside goes red. Like wine. It means we're in for a sharp winter.'

The wind picked up, and I wanted to catch a leaf. I could remember seeing my mother and father doing this when they were younger, running and laughing in a gale. I asked them about it once, but neither could remember it happening. The more I enthused, reminding them how much they had laughed and danced, the more uneasy they looked.

When I caught a plum coloured leaf, I risked biting into it, tasting for the sugar. It was disappointing to find that it tasted like grass.

Felling the orchard, and burning the stumps took less time than Dad thought it would, so on Bonfire night, he promised me a swimming pool. It wasn't the first time he'd suggested it, but now he said it would happen, because he had time on his hands. I sneered. I can't remember the phrase I used, but it was a ten year old boy's equivalent to, 'I'll believe it when I see it.'

I'd only been hit twice before, but I expected it to happen then, because it was a cruel thing to say.

'You rotten little bugger,' he said softly. The white in his eyes went red, not with anger, but with tears, making the iris look all the more blue. Until that moment, if somebody had asked, I wouldn't have known what colour his eyes were.

When I woke up the next morning, the plot was staked out, nylon string pegged in a rectangle. In those days, it was unusual for anyone to think of owning a swimming pool unless they were rich. This was a special treat, and I felt bad for suggesting he couldn't do it. But not bad enough to apologise.

It wouldn't be a covered pool, and the water wouldn't be heated. Being about the size of our front room there wouldn't be much swimming, and keeping leaves out would be a battle, but it was more than anybody else had in Calne.

My sleep became as weak as Dad's, and I woke to the sound of him digging each morning, then sat at the window watching him. What looked like a small area of land, seemed huge when you saw how small each lump of soil was.

He could have hired the summer staff for a couple of week-ends, to help out, but he wanted to do it all himself. When it was getting deep enough to look worthwhile, it filled with three inches of tea coloured water. Then it turned to ice, and there was nothing he could do except wait.

*

We opened for camping in March, but the pool was unfinished. Although Dad had been working on it since the thaw – smoothing the sides, building a breeze-block shed for the filter-pump, connecting the pipes – the hole itself was no deeper. I heard him call it an eyesore one night, and hoped he would be able to complete it. I wasn't desperate to go swimming, but I couldn't face seeing him disappointed. If we reached November, something would happen to remind him of the year before. A smell or sound, would remind him of the night he offered me something special to hope for, and he would remember the way I reacted.

Walking between the tents, listening to the chug and hiss of Calor stoves, I was glad for the visitors who came here. They were ordinary people, with jobs, and yet they felt it was worth paying my Dad to sleep outside, in the cold and rain, cooking Pot Noodles and soup. Sometimes they drove into town to the chippie, but I could tell from the way they hid their chip papers afterwards that it made them feel guilty. My favourite time was around ten o'clock in the morning, when the sun was high enough to dry most of the water from the tents. Only a few drops remained, and as the campers re-pegged their canvas, making the glossy material taught, those slid down the sides, the trails evaporating as I watched.

It was the best opportunity I've ever have to meet so many people, but I didn't want to talk, only to observe. Sitting by the edge of the pool, which was dry to the point of cracking by August, I was sometimes approached by the more elderly campers. The ones who wanted to talk were usually wearing shorts, with bare bellies, covered in white hair, one towel over their shoulder. Between the tents and the toilet block, they stopped to ask me what the hole was for.

'Are you helping your Dad out then?'

'I don't think so.'

'You should put your back into it.'

I didn't even help in the shop, because Mum was too soft to ask me. If I helped at all, tidying the cans on the shelf, sorting out tickets for new arrivals, she treated me to extra pocket money. I knew what I was doing, sitting back and letting my parents work so hard, but I tried to kid myself that their red faces were a sign of health, rather than exhaustion.

That summer, Dad bought a new refrigerator for the shop, with clear glass doors, so the visitors could see lines of cold cans and bottles. He was so proud, showing me the motor at the back, the solder joints, explaining how the exchange system worked. He was right, in that it helped to sell drinks, but it gave off so much heat that all our fresh food went bad quickly, and we had to keep the windows open until closing time.

'I'm not sure this thing was a good idea,' Dad said to me after a week. 'Too much heat. It gets in the way.'

The next morning he was up earlier than ever, and when I opened the curtains, he stopped digging, looked around and waved. It was the only time he ever did that, which makes me think it might have been a dream. There was no way he could have heard me sitting up in bed, or seen the curtains moving. He was smiling, because the hole was much bigger than it should have been. In one go he'd cleared out more earth than he'd managed in the previous week.

*

If he'd asked me to help, I might have done, but it was never even suggested. I sat out with him more often, though, especially at night. When it was quiet outside, going cold, the house lights looked inviting, but we stayed out, Dad mixing one more load of concrete.

When the sides had been reinforced and plastered, he painted them with a blue rubber solution. It was like a skin he said, that could stretch without cracking. When set it felt like touching a hard inner-tube, drying the oil from my hands, making the skin uncomfortably tight.

I made sure I never asked Dad how long it would take to finish the pool, and he never offered an estimate. This probably made me look less than enthusiastic, and I couldn't think of a way to convince him that I was pleased, without putting pressure on him.

On a cool day in mid-August, Dad dragged a hose pipe up to the pool. I was sitting on the edge, my feet dangling over the light blue space, and I could see it was an effort for him not to smile. The pipe was already switched on, making glugging noises, but he lowered it into the pool before the water came out. When it did, the even paint made it difficult to see the liquid.

'This bloody weather,' he said, then, as an afterthought, 'There, I told you I'd do it.'

'Yeah, thanks. How long will it take to fill?'

He shook his head walking off. 'I don't know.'

Having upset him again, I decided to stay with the hose until the pool was full, but after two hours, it was only a foot deep. In all that time, only one camper came to see what was going on. The man was younger than most; the father of a family who were packing their tent, and he smelt of sun tan lotion, even on a day like this. He asked me if the pool would be open to the public next year.

'No, it's for me.'

'That's a waste of water isn't it?'

I went in for tea at five, and my Dad said, 'You don't want to be eating if you're going for a swim. Or is it too cold for you?'

'No, it's fine.'

'Is it full yet?'

'It's getting there.'

I was lying, because after a whole afternoon it was only about four feet deep.

'Let's go and have a look.'

I went with him, dreading the word 'leak'. He never said it, but accepted that was probably as deep as it was going to get.

'That good enough for you?'

The water felt like melted ice cubes, but it was deep enough to float in it. I shivered, and pushed myself backwards. Air that felt warm and still before I got in, now felt like cold wind on my wet skin.

'How is it?' Dad asked, kneeling at the edge.

'Great.'

He dipped his hand in, leaving it there for a few seconds, making me think he wanted a swim. I should have asked him to join me. He would have laughed, and said yes, eventually, and gone to get his trunks; but he said, 'It feels cold.'

'No, it's not. It's fine.'

When he was gone, I floated again, trying to let the water become as still as a bath. It took a long time, made more difficult by trying to control my breathing and avoiding the edges, without making ripples. The high edges meant that I couldn't see anything except the blue sides, and cloud. I didn't even know which way I was facing. I could make out sounds – the hammering of ten pegs, spoons scraping food from pans, flushing from the toilet block – but they echoed off the sides making their direction uncertain.

Mum came out to have a look, standing at the edge with her arms folded.

'You be careful,' she said. 'Don't fall asleep.'

If she'd felt the temperature, she would have been thinking of pneumonia rather than sleep. She was joined by Dad, and after they had looked at me for a while, they started talking about something else, looking over the campsite, and I realised it was the first time in ages I'd seen them have a conversation, that wasn't to do with work. Neither was making excuses to the other, no tasks were being set, or complaints made; they were just talking.

'You'd better come in, it's getting cold,' Mum said.

When I was out, Dad sprinkled chlorine dust on the surface. It looked like chalk, but fizzed as it hit, melting into the water, smelling like a real swimming pool.

The water filter had to be on for a few hours each day, but because of my floating, Dad agreed to switch it on when I was elsewhere. We used this time to add extra water, which was a daily requirement.

Obtaining stillness wasn't the only thing I did in the pool. Sometimes I tried to swim without scraping my knees, and I risked a few surface dives. For a while I played at recovering coins from the bottom, which helped me learn to control my breathing. Most of all, though, I enjoyed lying on the surface on cloudy days. This gave my body two temperatures; the cold on my back, and the relative warmth of air on my chest, legs and face. One movement of my arms could slop the cold on to the warmth. If I was completely still, and held my breath, the water next to my skin warmed up; one deep breath would swirl it away.

Bad habits can stay with you for years. Not just habits of satisfaction, such as smoking, or scab picking, but habits of thought. Cynical habits, the habit of mistrust and anger, can be so firm, they are a strain to break, even when you recognise the problem. Why is it that good habits desert you so readily?

A few weeks after I started school again, I lost interest in the pool. It wasn't much cooler, but I made excuses to stay away from it. When leaves sat on its surface, then saturated and sank, I thought of it as a dirty place. Dad turned the filter off for winter, and let the level drop.

Some time in November, during a Chemistry lesson, we sublimated a solid to gas in a test tube. It was heavy, like the smoke

of a match in an ash tray. The gas contained chlorine, and sniffing it, I thought I was fainting, floating on my back. Nobody in
class noticed my reaction, but I spent the rest of the day feeling
tired, the way you do before catching a cold.

When I got home that night, I went to look at the pool. There
was a plank leading from the bottom to the edge, put there
because frogs were living in it now, and Dad thought they might
drown.

'The sides are so high,' he said. 'We don't want dead frogs
when it's time to clean it up.'

That was the reassurance I wanted, that the pool wasn't
abandoned, merely postponed.

In January, after the first frozen night, I climbed on to the
pool's ice, clinging on to the ledge above head height, sliding
around the edge, breaking ice behind me. The next day it had
refrozen, my destruction from the previous day welded on to
the new ice. When it thawed out, the water was thicker than
before.

It took Dad two mornings to clear it out, scooping the slime
out, a bucket full at a time. The blue paint was cracked in places,
because the concrete had ruptured too severely for it to cope. He
filled the gaps, repainted them, and scrubbed the floor.

When we tried to switch the filter on, it made a strained
sound, then jammed. It was a huge contraption, with several
sections. We looked in the metallic blue barrel first, but couldn't
find anything amiss. Then Dad unhooked a clasp that secured
the pipe filter. It was designed to stop large objects, such as
leaves, making it through to the sand filter. Inside, there was a
mass of something like coiled seaweed. Dad pulled his hands
away in shock, and I was able to see that the green lines were
frogs, sucked together, and stretched around each other. Their
breathing betrayed life, but they weren't able to move.

'We didn't turn it on, we didn't turn it on,' he said. 'We can't
have sucked them in. Not in that short a time.'

I couldn't work out how the frogs managed to get up the
pipe, or why they were in the pool at all since Dad had cleaned
it. Surely, they couldn't have been in the pipe since then. Their
legs looked much longer than they should have done, but from
what I could see, no skin was broken.

'Should we get Mum?' I asked.

'No, no, I'll sort this out.' A minute later he was still looking into the pump, where the frogs were moving more than before. I was starting to panic, because they were in pain.

'Perhaps they'll make it out on their own,' he said.

I was distressed, because I could see them suffering, too weak to pull free, but my protest upset Dad even more.

'Do it yourself. Go on. Go on.'

He said it with such force that I stuck my hand in, trying to flick the frogs, rather than touch them. When I brushed their skin, I felt the muscles bunch up, and I couldn't go any further.

'Get your Mum, then.'

Before bed, I washed my hands with Zest soap until they smelt of nothing but lemons. The sensation of damaged frogs was still there, but worse was the memory of seeing my Mum stick her hand in and pull the creatures free. I watched from a good distance, so there wasn't much I could make out. It wasn't the frogs that bothered me, but the look on her face. She didn't like it any more than we did, but she was getting on with it anyway.

*

When it was running again, I returned to floating. My concentration wasn't the same at first, and I became cold too easily, but I kept trying. By midsummer I was able to float for hours at a time, without the cold making my breathing too difficult. The only long term effect was that my fingers were numb most of the time, whiter than normal.

I never fell asleep in the pool, but it often happened the other way around; I would dream of floating. Half asleep in the morning, I would think I was in the pool. Sometimes, I could even smell the chlorine, because the window was open.

I like to think that if Mum hadn't become ill, we could have keep the pool going for years. Even when she first went into hospital, I thought there was a chance. The pool was something that could bring me and Dad together, help us through a difficult time. There were too many demands on our time though. When you miss one sprinkling of chlorine, you may as well give up. It only takes a few days for the water to discolour and thicken.

We were both coping well, I thought. Neither of us was really upset. We got on with running the campsite, keeping things moving. When it was under control, Dad even talked about redecorating the bedroom, as a surprise for Mum when she came home. I would have offered to help, but I knew nothing about it.

*

I honestly believed that Mum's absence wasn't having an effect on me, until Dad upset himself trying to cook something in the microwave. It was a ready-made meal, pasta blobs stuffed with cheese. He put the food in a dish, and heated it, confused when it came out cracked and hard. By the time he asked for my help, he'd ruined three bowls full.

'You add water first,' I said.

'Oh, oh, of course.'

He's not thick, not absent-minded even, and that's what upset me. If he was just being stupid, I would have laughed, we'd probably have laughed together. It wasn't stupidity, but weakness. I think he was trying as hard as I was not to cry.

Mum was in hospital much longer than we expected, and it was horrible getting used to the thought of her as an old, ill person. In a matter of weeks, that's how we came to see her. I make an effort to remember her up and about, doing things in the shop, watching over me in the water, but it's much easier to picture her in bed, tense and bony.

The doctors sent her home to recover, so they were as surprised as we were when, after two brief days of telling us not to fuss, she relapsed. The last time I saw her, she was so far down in bed that her head was resting below the pillows. Her eyes were sleepy but open, mouth closed. I don't know if she was dead at that point, because the sequence of events is muddled, but I remember the look on her face. It was calm, but thoughtful. Perhaps my face looked the same to her, when she watched me floating, worried that I was asleep.

'It's a shame about that,' Dad said one afternoon, when I was standing by the pool side, still in my school uniform, not wanting to go inside. The water was black, some form of mould growing up the sides. 'We could do it up again in the spring.'

I wanted to say yes, to thank him for the pool, tell him how much I enjoyed being in there, but couldn't get the words out. He probably thought I was sulking, looking down into the pit, but I was trying to find a way to tell him what it was like for me. Closing my eyes, I remembered floating, feeling light and cold and happy. When I opened them, I was alone.

Pilotage

Most people don't know what the stars are. Bits of planets, comets, meteors, asteroids, space dust. They might as well believe in the music of the spheres. Ask what makes stars shine, and they say, 'Light from the Sun?' Watch their faces change when you tell them that every star is a sun, hundreds of times wider than the earth, crushing itself into nuclear fury. You probably knew that already, but most people don't. I often wonder how they get through the day.

I don't hate anyone for being ordinary, because the most racist and dull people occasionally wake up. Even those who find pleasure in shopping can move me, when something forces them to change. There's been more of that recently, though not of all of it's positive.

There's a lot of anger in Barrow, some of it towards Vickers, most towards the Tories. People even spit about money itself. Walking round town is like being in a Panorama documentary, or a Ken Loach film. Social realism. When people fight, it's not just to get it out of their system, it's to hurt their opponent. There's no cunning involved, no need to ask if a pint was spilled or a stare established, the fighting simply evolves from the presence of people. There's a rage that can only be relieved by flattening somebody else, making them still. These urban myths about people sucking eyes out, and using taped-together Stanley knives (so the wound won't knit), they all originate here.

I was taught that anger and hatred come from a fear of stasis, but in Barrow, people are angry because they know things are changing for the worse. It should really be on the news, the way it's going. There are so many people out of work, young and old, that the whole place stinks of piss and booze. Getting to the dole queue is made tricky by the puddles of sick that coat the footpaths on a midweek morning. Everything gets tackier, troubled by another layer of scum. The kids grow up vicious and gobby, and nobody gives a shit. I'm told its the same everywhere, but although my experience is limited, I can't quite accept that's the case.

There is always tension here, because everything revolves around the submarines, which are – to say the least – volatile. They fire up the reactors inside that fifty-foot concrete slab, before slipping them into the sea. Nobody talks about safety, because nobody believes in it. When we get outsiders in the pubs, asking about the submarines – and Heysham to the south, Sellafield to the north – we try to stop them going too far. They tell us it's the most radioactive coastline in the world, ask us about acceptable levels. That's not something we care to chat about.

There's a saying about living on the edge, which locals use from time to time. Visitors assume it's something to with the fear of an explosion. In truth, it used to refer to living on the coast, building at town against the waves, but now it sums up the poverty. The whole place is one great bargain bin. Don't ask the price, everything's 50p.

Some good comes out of all this. Barrow may appear to be slumped, but inside, everybody's cooking. That energy has to go somewhere.

Sometimes I follow drunken people, and listen to their speeches. Whether they walk in groups, singing, or chant to themselves, they talk mostly in gibberish, slang and obscenity. If you listen for long enough, somebody will move to a higher level and say something mystical. It might not mean anything to them at the time, or will be lost by morning, but for me, these words are treasure.

You see people acting in imaginative ways when they're in a state. The rage of a man walking home, pissed off, pissed up, dangerously upset about the way Jennifer chatted to Steven, is a potent force, an energy that shouldn't be wasted. Sometimes they walk on the ledge of Jubilee bridge, over to Walney island, not for bravado, but because they want to scare themselves. It's not the alcohol; it's the decision to step aside from the ordinary for a while. You might call it reckless, but I see it as empowerment. It's impossible for that sort of action to go unnoticed; it changes the world.

*

When I met Katie Oswald, she was eighteen years old, pumping petrol at the Lucas garage, on the north coast road at Barrow in Furness. It was a summer of cloud and mist and heat. Nobody was sunburnt, but we all went brown, progressively dyed by the light. We'd squinted for two months against the stiff air, storing white in the creases around our eyes. At night, when relaxed, the lines came into view. The sun was always merging with the fuzz around it. Although there were areas of blue sky, it never opened up to the wide bowl that it can do in flat lands. Except on the day we met. The clouds collected over the horizon of the Lake District, sucking on to the mountains, leaving the sky over Barrow as bare and blue as winter. The sea is grey at best, sometimes black with sewage, but on the ninth it reflected the sky, giving the illusion of Mediterranean waters. The sun was clear and sparkly. Staring up at it that morning, I realised why children draw it with rays all around it. When your eyes water, the light spreads out of it that way.

Katie turned nineteen, and was upset when her squint lines became permanent. Having been free of oil and spots for less than a year, it was distressing to lose her youthful sap. She spent more time looking at those lines than she did at the good parts of her body. The more they grew, the more she rubbed in potions and cream. There was so much to celebrate about her body, I'll never know why she focused on the problem areas.

We were all withered by summer, but nobody cared as much as Katie. It was probably her fixation with the surface of things, that made her look to me for help.

*

It's difficult to recognise a moment of change. Some people would have you believe that your whole life is defined by the way mummy wiped your arse the first time. If you end up beating children and screaming at traffic, it's nothing to do with what's happening, it's all down to anal pressure. Others say we're fluid, changing according the whims of circumstance, so there's no such thing as personality.

Neither of these theories satisfy me, or agree with the facts. People are set in their ways, speaking in phrases, waking up in the same mood, eating the same sandwiches; but everybody can change.

There's usually an accident, revelation, or illness, some extreme which gives you the option of lability. You could say this is a response to circumstance, but I believe it's down to a willingness to look. When people open up to the world, it comes inside. The change isn't always instantaneous, but it is persistent. The past is like slow poison; our sly attempts at metabolism fuel its potency.

They say that astronauts come back with heads full of figures and procedures and process, but inside, they are stained by the experience. The size of the earth stays with them, and whether they chose religion or seclusion, everything has changed.

For Katie Oswald, change came from the drip feed of observation.

The Lucas garage is situated on a bend in the road, pushing it against the coast. She sat in the cabin, behind her cash register, rocking back on the stool, watching the forecourt. When she was outside with a customer, leaning away from the worst of the fumes, she looked over the beach and sea to the northern length of Walney Island. There were two hangers, a control tower, the clubhouse, and a couple of caravans. By the side of these, the red wind-sock was stiffened by a westerly. It was too distant to see people, and the runways were hidden in wild grass, their presence marked out to her by the aircraft that flew on to them.

It was a quiet airfield, most of its traffic being from the soaring club. A single glider was dragged into the sky by an orange tug plane, then set to fall. During the week flights were brief, and sometimes it was taken up twenty times a day. She couldn't see the cable that connected the aircraft while they were that high, and it looked as though the glider was formation flying. When the latch was released, the tug diving to the right, the glider climbing to the left, she could see the tension between them break.

The glider changed shape in the turns, from white to a black needle, reforming as it swooped around. Sometimes she would lose sight of it completely, until it came in on finals, rectangular flaps jutting out of the wings. There was a throbbing sound and a hiss. She thought it must be the same with all aeroplanes; the wings are singing, but you never hear them because of the engine.

Back in the cabin, she smelt liquorice, melting chocolate, oil and polish. It was always there, but her senses were coming to.

On hotter days, when the clouds crafted themselves to storm size, the glider circled beneath, taken up by rising air. When it was cool, with wind from the west, it flew out to Black Combe – the first mountain of the Lake District – gaining lift from the ridge winds. If the air was still, as it was for much of that summer, she saw the glider home in on Vickers, using heat from the submarine house to buffet itself higher.

The Saturday after we met, she worked late, given the responsibility of locking up and taking the keys home with her. For the first time, she stayed on until dark. The forecourt gave off warmth and the petrol smelt clean. There were two floodlights on either side of the garage, each cancelling out the other's shadows. She stayed outside, enjoying the lack of customers. She could hear the sea, and spotted the tug plane, coming back with the tow rope, releasing it on to the strip before vanishing in touch down.

The glider's flight was short, diving straight back into the circuit because it was getting too dark.

Katie didn't know, but the pilot wasn't trained for night flying. He was using the legal limit of the daytime flying definition, to squeeze in his last flight. As he came in, the fog of town light contrasted against the island, so that he couldn't make out the airfield's features. All he could see was black. The tower was closed for the night, making it invisible, apart from the red tip of its aerial. The runway lights were rarely in use, so he used the coast road and compass to get his bearings. Within the dark, he saw the tyre-scratched numbers for runway 35. It was difficult to judge distance, so he flew in over the numbers, and as they slid beneath him, brought the glider level, losing the horizon in the round out. Knowing he could still be twenty feet up, he pulled into a stall.

I was watching from outside the clubhouse. The tug pilot was oblivious because he taxied to the hanger door, killed the engine, and was winding on the wheel-brace to drag his aeroplane inside, while Patrick was flying blind towards the unseen runway. I looked at the hanger, the tail of the plane moving inside, then back to the glider. He was flying slowly, flaps on full, but pitched in steep. I thought he was getting it all wrong, flying into the ground, but he was using the angle to get a better view. When he lifted for the stall, he was too high, but not dangerously so. The drop gave him momentum, so that after the first impact, he ballooned, then came down again. The contact had helped him judge what was going on, if nothing else, and he kept it level. Being the last flight, he left the brakes off, using his speed to roll up the runway. By the time I reached him, the glider was coming to a halt, one wing dipping to the tarmac.

You really need three people to move a glider safely, but we were the only ones left, so we each took a wing handle, promising to keep it slow. There wasn't much we wanted to say, until the glider was manoeuvred into place, and then we leaned up against the hanger doors to force them shut. The tug pilot was leaving, his Land Rover driving so slowly we could have run to catch up, but we let him go.

Should we walk then, I said, knowing there was no other option. It was more than two miles to my house, another ten minutes for Patrick, but he agreed. We should leave our bikes in the control tower, I thought, or I should drive more often, because this wasn't the first time we'd been last off the island.

It was warm as we walked, but the shock must have settled in Patrick, because he was struggling for breath.

Being parallel with the coast of Barrow, we looked over, and Patrick said he'd never been so glad to see it, as when he flew back in. He knew it could go dark quickly, but wasn't prepared for a rush of night. Without the familiar shape of the town, he would have been completely lost. One of the lights at the Lucas garage was turned off, and Patrick watched with me, as the other went out. He repeated his comment about never being so glad and went quiet.

*

Katie Oswald watched television in bed, until the electric meter ran out. She'd been channel hopping anyway. There was no point in getting up to renew the meter, because until morning she wouldn't need electricity. The fridge would be off, but it needed defrosting anyway. There was more ice than food in there.

The television screen retained a phosphorescent sheen. Staring directly at it, she could see almost nothing, but when she looked away it appeared like a flash. Her reaction was to stare straight back at it, which made it vanish. The rhythm of her pupils from side to side wearied her eyes, and they closed.

Human eyes are uncommonly sensitive. The minute energy of a single photon can register as light. When astronauts try to sleep, their retinas are bombarded by a background radiation that never reaches earth. Each particle activates an individual cell, appearing as a speck of bright; the effect is similar to staring at a television filled with static.

Katie saw a brownish, sludgy pattern moving chaotically, unaffected when she opened and closed her eyes. It would be satisfying to see nothing, but the mottling remained. This reminded her of being sent to bed early, when she would relieve the boredom by pressing her palms into her eyes sockets, causing patterns to appear. By squashing the *vitreous humor* against the retina, she excited the cells. Imagination played a part, twisting the entoptics into frames of colour and structure. She could have tried this again, but instead observed the rusty darkness, wondering if was a defect caused by her childhood habit.

Drifting in and out of sleep, her dreams were dull and repetitive. Waking frequently, she was aware that time was passing, unsure of its rate. When the window filled with blue, she guessed it must be around five o'clock. The colour of dawn is an illusion; in reality, all the colours are present, but our eyes are incapable of picking them up. The cells which respond to red are less efficient; the world appears blue because that colour is easier to see at low intensity.

It would be misleading to say that she felt fully rested, because her sleep had been too disturbed, but she didn't feel as shattered as usual. Sleep was a paradox, something she forced herself to do when wide awake, which left her feeling tired. According to convention, it was supposed to be the other way round.

That morning, her eyes were free of crust, hair feeling clean. When she dressed, her clothes slid over her flesh without any feel of stickiness. In the mirror, nothing had changed, but she found she was rubbing her hands together, the vigour making her uncomfortable.

*

The renewal is frequently accompanied by restlessness, a desire to do something extreme. For Patrick, his moment of opening was so unusual, it left him desperate.

Nobody can suggest where the change in him began, but one afternoon in 1984 can be singled out as the time when the alteration became tangible.

Working part-time in two different pubs, while collecting a giro, Patrick's needs were few. He lived with his parents to save money, using most of his wage to keep flying. His other luxury was a red Fiesta, but on this he spent as little as possible. He believed that leaving petrol in the tank was wasteful, that twenty billion gallons of fuel were sloshing unused in cars every day. What's the point of leaving a fiver's worth below the red line, he said, if you can run it to empty and get your money's worth. So he carried a plastic can of fuel in front of the passenger seat, waiting for the familiar stutter and cessation of the engine.

At first this was nothing more than an inconvenience, as normal to him as refuelling at a petrol station, but in time it became a form of divination. Wherever he ran out, it felt as though he was being shown something. The code of these locations was unclear to him. Sometimes he came to a halt in the middle of a blind bend, or on a bridge, and although there could be obvious symbology, he believed there was something more subtle to it.

He charted the locations on a map, to see if there was any correlation. Some of them did line up, but less spectacularly than he hoped. It was possible there was no code, only the location itself. He was being shown a place, for the sake of looking at it.

When you've lived in the same area for years, driving on certain roads becomes automatic; there are clear reference points that guide your driving. You know there are some places where it's safe to look at the hills, or watch the sky. Other than that, all you see is tarmac, fencing, hedges, and the distinctive litter – shoes, tyres and baby bottles – of the roadside. If somebody else makes you a passenger, the same road becomes new. Where you normally watch the cats eyes curve around a bend, you can look to the left, and see highland cattle in a paddock you didn't know was there. Or a canal beneath a bridge, which you thought went over a railway line. Or a ploughed field, coated with the smut of bone meal and milt, its powder shining like swarf. For Patrick, interruptions to his journey were the same. He was being given an excuse to pause and observe. While the petrol ran into the tank, he was given a few seconds to take in his surroundings.

The needle was unreliable; it could fall to its lowest point an hour before the last drops were used, or with a few minutes to spare. On some journeys, Patrick would take the scenic route, to ensure that he didn't make it home without a reason to stop. That September, he went further out of his way, coaxing an event into being. He wasn't supposed to be driving, because they had taken his wisdom teeth out that morning. The anaesthetic turned his blood to something like anti-freeze, icy and sour, leaving him shaky. The only discomfort came from a strain in his jaw and the memory of clamps under his lips, so he refused the offer of codeine, in case it wearied him further. With his wounds dry, able to speak normally, he convinced them he was being picked up.

He didn't want to go straight home, so went out of town to the east, curving back towards Barrow from the north. When the engine hesitated, caught, then faltered, he knew that this stoppage would be special, because it wasn't a road he was familiar with, and the car rolled to a halt in a lay by. When it was refuelled, he locked up and walked away, wanting to see more than the obvious location.

The fields were delineated by barbed wire and gates, but there were no hedges. The footpath he located had no signpost, and could have been private. Walking without a hedge made him feel exposed.

The ache left his muscles, and the after-effects of his operation gave him a feeling of resilience. He looked back for the car, but it was out of sight, no sign of the road. In all directions, he could only see the fields, most set-aside, some containing over-ripe wheat, the heads drooping.

Behind the banking, he found a river, which the path now adhered to. The stillness made it look like a winding canal, its varnished surface well below the banking. There didn't appear to be any variation in depth, and although the sun showed up a fine suspension of silt, he could see no fish, stones or rocks. There was none of the usual detritus of litter, grass and plastic around the river; the banked edges were too smooth and steep, with no rushes for materials to gather on.

Down the exact centre of the river, cutting ripples around itself, a smoking log floated towards him. It was a thick branch, the ends snapped rather than cut, its bark turned into charcoal.

It moved without sound, smoke coming out of the cracks. The log rotated around its length in front of him, betraying currents, settling again on its axis, following the curve of the river. When it was past him he smelt the burn of it, like water poured on a still-warm bonfire. Looking upriver, he could see the stretch of fields, pylons, distant farm buildings. There were no fires, factories, or trees, no smoke or activity to show where it could have come from.

The clouds were thin, but dark, untouched by low sunlight, which made the landscape brighter. The pylons turned the colour of bulb filaments, the grasses beneath them over exposed. A scent of burning remained, but the log had gone, the water recreating flatness.

By the time Patrick made it back to his car, the sun had fused over with even stratus and he was shivering. Already restless, he drove back faster than he needed to, knowing something had to be done.

*

While Katie was coming to terms with her renewal, I was struggling through the heat of morning, reconnoitring the streets around my home. It was late summer, so I tried not to resent the weather. The temperature was pleasant, but I was sick of the unrelenting dazzle of clouds.

We don't perceive the real intensity of light, otherwise the brilliance of a summer sun at midday would baffle us, and we would be blind as moles at night. It's the ratios that count, the way one state relates to another. We can read by the light of a single candle, or just as easily by the sun, which is a hundred thousand times stronger. Step into a dark room, and the eye manufactures visual purple; move outside and, a brown pigment floods the cells, protecting them from overload. This keeps our eyes safe, but it takes a while to adjust between these states.

At night, pubs are all you can see in the middle of town, their windows spangled with bottle light. During the day, they blend in amongst the shops, like foreign banks. You see them, but they don't register. If you've ever been inside a pub first thing in the morning, before opening time, amongst the polish and ash you can see traces of anger. When the sunlight's ripping through, it reveals webs in the air, rippled like heat haze. That's where the world's been damaged by somebody's pain.

Ian McKenna's parents ran The Lamb; we weren't friends, but I'd known him since he as in the fourth year at school, which meant I was served easily at night, and could return in the mornings to clear up the remains. He never trusted me fully, and wandered in and out of the main lounge, on the pretext of moving a chair or distributing beer-mats. He must have had this image of me slotting myself beneath a gin dispenser and opening the valve. The truth is more mundane; I was clearing up the worst harm, and I preferred privacy. Each time he came into the room, I could do nothing other than look shifty. When he was gone, it gave me only a few moments to soften my eyes, locate the fractures, and heal.

I explained this to Ian several times, but he believed there was something vampiric about it, as though I was stealing energy to use in a ritual. I could never get it through to him that ritual has little meaning for me. It can break inertia, but nothing more.

Even so, he was co-operative, and let me go through the process without a single refusal. The eagerness with which he let me in made me think he might have been afraid, not of myself, but of leaving pain in his building.

Ian tried not to look at me when he opened the door. He was dressed, but I got the impression from his tired face and the smell of smoke, that he'd been up all night. Inside, I was shocked by the extent of the damage; it wasn't visible at this point, because I hadn't adjusted my eyes, but I could tell there was a large disruption. I asked him about the previous night; I'd left early, around eight o'clock, but had anything happened after that?

Nothing exciting, he said, apart from a brawl with the police, but that was outside.

No arguments, somebody crying, a person sitting alone?

Nothing. That he could remember.

I pointed to the alcove, around the main fireplace, relaxing my eyes. A fibre of pain was strung into the air, spreading like a glass lily, coated in oil, so clear I thought he would be able to see it. Something had happened there, I assured him. It was easy to catch sight of it, even while I was talking. He moved his hand around his face, which I mistook for a signal, but he was rubbing his ginger beard; it meant he was thinking. He couldn't remember anything, he said, pulling the longer hairs with his finger tips. The other hand gripped his Guinness towel. He was probably wondering if he should ask me to leave. Instead, I asked him to.

When alone, I moved toward the distortion. It became blurred, so I looked to the side bringing it into focus. It's the same technique you use for watching dim stars. If you stare at them they disappear, because the core of your retina is tuned for bright detail, rather than night vision. By looking to the side, using a different part of your eye, the smallest stars are available. The skill is to shift your concentration from the obvious centre.

The sunlight was diffuse and cloudy, but where it seeped through the distortion, it sharpened like chrome. A wise person would have closed the wound at once, but I was tempted by its grandeur. Whatever conniption had brought this into the world, would be of interest. And there was something familiar about its structure that made me want to read it.

There's nothing dangerous about moving into the threads; the worst that can happen is that you'll resonate with the pain and make it grow. You've probably felt this, passing through the scene of a previous argument. It returns, soils your mood, and the room becomes unpleasant, but that's all. Touching the fibres with the intent of sipping memories, isn't usually risky, but our real aim is to contain the event. Sometimes there's nothing more than a smell or a word. Occasionally you see the person who released the distortion, the event of their pain, as the thread is taken in and stored.

This one revealed nothing at first, making me feel numb and nervous, as though something was missing. It was like looking in a mirror and seeing myself standing ten feet further back.

Until then, it hadn't occurred to me that the fracture could have been placed there deliberately.

*

There's no way a person can go this deeply into healing, without a retreat. You need a place to unravel the threads of disorder. It's not that we use the pain as fuel for our workings, even though pain is an essential part of it. We aren't feeding off the damage, so much as clearing it out. Carrying a month's worth of chaos dampens your mood, which is why we need the rage. It restores stability. Any benefits we receive are a by-product.

Nobody talks about what might happen if the pain was left inside, without the cleansing of rage. That's like asking what would happen if you stopped going to the toilet. It's more likely to be messy than interesting.

It's usually on a Wednesday evening when the airfield is quiet, that we gather inside the clubhouse at dusk. That's about the only symbol we permit; twilight is a time of change. There's no elected hierarchy, no order of arrival, though I'm often the first. For me, the process begins the moment I leave my front door.

Once together, there is no ritual or invocation, no salt circle or scratched symbols. We use silence to release the anger.

Under normal circumstances, people are incapable of obtaining silence. Even when the creak of your guts fades, and traffic and breeze and floorboards are made quiet, you can hold your breath, still your heart, and there will remain a perception of sound. A humming tone, sometimes a whistle. These illusory whispers are the result of damage to the inner ear, caused by sounds so loud or tenacious, they have weakened a part of the cochlea that responds to them. As punishment, a trace of that vibration stays with you forever; it's the auditory version of a phantom limb. Age-related deafness is nothing to do with quiet, but the roar of past noises brought together at once. The collective memory of sound drowns out the detail of speech.

If you listen for long enough, while you drop off, this background rumble turns into music, singing voices and violins. It can wake you up, or be lost as you fall asleep.

In our stillness, the same would happen, which is why even this frothing of our damaged ears must be checked, by use of the imagination. Once the rage is underway sound returns, but to set it in motion we need absolute silence. The others senses need not be restrained, which is fortunate, because the clubhouse is rich in all of them. From the outside, it looks like a sagging shed, every panel showing more grey wood than paint. Inside, it is essentially a single room, containing one table and several chairs. Two of the walls are windowless, the other two made almost entirely of glass. From the west we can see the last of the light coming over the sea, across the airfield. To the east there is the bridge to Barrow, and the docks. The walls are adorned with aeroplane posters, maps and charts. It smells of floorboards and rice paper. As the twilight thickens, the posters and hangings lose their detail, the gloss on them reflecting like blurred mirrors. For our workings, the table is moved to the side, the chairs arranged in a circle, facing in.

The others usually arrive in cars, their headlights splintering in the grime of the windows. Donald Beyer, Nellie Francis, Beryl Carney and Nick Gavaurin. Upon entering, they let in sea air, then shut it out. Each successive closure lessens the volume. Patrick is the last to arrive, and he comes in smelling of tobacco and garlic from the pizza parlour.

When we are all present, with the quiet established, we make eye contact, one to the other, before becoming still. Outside, it is dark, but our vision is catching up, and there's enough lambency from Barrow to keep us visible.

Each month the responsibility of being the victim is passed round clockwise. Whoever is chosen walks to the centre of the room, facing the direction of their chair.

Initiating the event takes an act of will, in much the same way that blinking or moving your arm does. There's more than decision involved, but no effort. The victim is willing to accept our pain, and without force, we let it go.

As the threads move out, it's important to concentrate on the victim. If you dwell on the pain, it can snag as it withdraws, leaving a vestige of distress that will linger for weeks. By losing everything to the rage, you avoid contamination.

Although the victim is always visibly moved by the event, when it's Patrick, the effects are more obvious. You see his hands cramping against themselves (which is why we keep our nails short), setting into fists. He makes steps to the left and right, sometimes backwards, always staring at his fingers, which open and close with the waves of fury. His teeth are tight, lips drawn back above and below, the strain in his face making the muscles solid. His arms move away from his body and back with each clench; it's as though he's is embracing something invisible and difficult to hold. A frenzied growl comes from his lungs with each contraction.

When our rage has pooled in the victim, it needs to be dispersed, so we give it direction, apply it in some way. By using the victim as an attractor, the others are unblemished, free to share and shape the power. This is why we've been accused of feeding off pain, which is less than fair. Our purpose is to remove the suffering from Barrow; if we gain benefits from this craft, as a side effect, who can complain?

*

Asking somebody out can be a callous act or a challenge, but sometimes it's tender and submissive. On the one hand you're focused of your desires, but on the other you're being selfless, giving yourself away, offering time and touch, concerned for the other's wishes.

You always ask somebody out with thought of pain. You want permission to unwrap your feelings, to play with them in the open, but equally, you want the other person to feel the same way; not for the convenience of your desires, but because you care. Rejection cannot tarnish your emotions, but unrequited love hurts because it means the world is a fraction more barren than you hoped.

The question, will you go out with me, really means will you hold me? Are you prepared to kiss me? Can we share skin? This is why it's a question that's rarely asked so directly. Instead we've developed a safety net of shared interest, where it's easier to ask somebody to spend time with them – in secondhand bookshops, pubs, bowling alleys, cinemas – using a veneer of friendship to build up accidental contact, working up to the first kiss. It occurs without a request, which is seen by most people as natural, more emotive than one person asking out the other.

I prefer the formality of a question, because although it may be contrived and old fashioned, it requires an honest answer. The sad thing is that, when Katie Oswald found the courage to ask me out, I couldn't bring myself to be truthful. There was too much at stake.

I'd used the tail end of two rage meetings to get a better look at Katie, to see how her observation was developing, but our physical meetings were few. I stood back while she put in the petrol, she looked out to sea, and then I handed her the money. Sometimes I'd give her a twenty, when I had the right change, so I could watch her walk to the cabin and come back to me, holding the change out as soon as she was outside. I would meet her half way, both of us hesitating, but rarely making conversation.

Patrick came with me the last few times, which was awkward, because she was becoming more confident. She talked to me about the airfield, asking about the gliders, the clubhouse, wondering who worked in the control tower. One day, she asked about the cost of flying, surprised it could be so cheap. Pointing at Patrick I told her that he was the chief instructor, and banged my hand on the roof. He didn't flinch, but stared over Walney at the approaching warm front, and Katie asked if he was all right. Concentrating on the light, I said, which was a clue, but I don't know whether she picked up on it.

A few hours later I went back, supposedly to top up, but it was really to see how she would react when I was alone. The speed with which she asked me out meant she must have been rehearsing it.

I know I don't know you, or anything, but would you go out with me?

While replacing my petrol cap, she could have followed that up with suggestions of places to go, things we could do, but she left it plain, which was enticing. The reason I said yes, however, was because I could see the depth of her awakening. Her face was appealing and I can't deny that I spent most of my time with her trying to gain an overview of her body, but this was aesthetic, desireless. My interest was practical. Before long she would be finding the pain of our town, and it was traditional to invite her into rage. If she was left to work it out for herself, she'd probably end up being her own victim.

*

Patrick is younger than me, so he learns quickly. His initiation came two years before mine, but he's even further ahead when you consider his age. We were both discovered by Donald Beyer, who runs the control tower on Walney. If it wasn't for his sleeveless shirts and khaki pants, Donald would look like an ageing doctor; long face, immaculate white hair, raised chin. I've never seen him smile or blink, the only betrayal of emotion comes when he swallows, his throat distended by a sharp Adam's apple. To an initiate, this calm makes Donald appear stronger than he is.

When Patrick was brought into the process, it was a couple of weeks after his experience by the river, and he was anxious for control. The way he clung to Donald during those first days – asking more questions than Don thought reasonable – may have led to his later isolation. Few of us are friends, coming together only for the rage, rarely discussing the nature of our activities. After his initial struggle, Patrick chose total isolation, letting go of his previous friends, moving away from his parents. It was only up the road, but he locked the door and refused to talk to them. All of this lessened when he met me, because he was no longer the beginner.

We soon established that the rage was something to be put aside when socialising, but we knew that without that connection we would never have been friends. By spending time together, we lessened the loneliness that keeping a secret brings.

There's something about newcomers that draws us to them. It's more than a sense of what they are, more than we gather from directed insights; coincidence brings them into our lives. Patrick was aware of me on several occasions, before I had any idea what was happening to me. When ever he saw me, he would approach, weigh me up, then back away.

He never told me about this, but I've looked at these moments, seen myself from his point of view. Once, he saw me observing a shadow that came off a lamp post. He could see that I was trying to work out the way the sun was shining, trying to see why the shadow had been spread in the middle, where it should have been precise.

Thinking back, I have no recollection of anybody else being in the street. If he had come to me then, and been my teacher, it's likely that we'd never have been friends. He held back from bringing it out in me, because of his age, letting Don stumble across me instead.

The awakening bothered me, because it was such a contrast to my previous state. Like many, I resisted for a while, until the sights that came to me were too intriguing to be ignored. When Donald found me, I was standing outside the paper mill, trying to follow a thread which tapered across the road to a bus stop.

He made himself known by walking into the rippled wire, absorbing the form into himself. Then he let me follow him to the clubhouse, where I was left to work most of it out for myself. Nothing was forced, and he refused to teach, in case his understanding polluted my discoveries.

In those early days I would hang around the airfield, trying to help with the gliding club, so that I could be near to the clubhouse, sometimes going to see Don, chatting with Patrick. I was never made welcome, until Patrick relented, and let me spend time with him. I think he was afraid of clinging, wanting me to be kind, but nervous about his desperation for my kindness.

It was rare for Patrick and myself to argue. We debated to the point of farce, but the subject matter was never personal or hurtful. In any debate, I would force an idea to its limit, even if it had no relation to my opinion, to see how malleable his belief could be. It's a regrettable habit, which has proved drastic in relationships. I end up sticking to a defensive argument that I have no belief in. The last person I was close to left me for that reason. The procedure's stayed with me, though, and this usually amuses Patrick. Our discussions were fierce, but we never argued with anger, so it was surprising when he chose a subject that annoyed me, and kept pushing with it.

He came with me to The Lamb, which was a curious location for him to try this, because it was known to be my territory. He began to goad me as soon as I'd paid for the first drinks.

Look at this, he said, pulling out a copy of *Nexus* magazine. There was no reason for him to be carrying that inside his jacket; he'd brought it with the sole intention of showing me. It bore headlines about the dangers of microwave ovens and fluoridation, hinting at conspiracy theories. I derided much of this, but he knew I was fond of saying that in amongst the disinformation, there was usually something worth knowing. I never bought the magazine myself, but I'd read many of his. The article he pointed out to me was one I wouldn't bother to read, claiming that the NASA space program was a myth.

I swore, which sounded strange coming from me. In a place like The Lamb, blasphemy gives speech its rhythm, but it's not something I care to use.

To prevent him getting the upper hand, I reminded him that this idea was gleaned from a seventies film. It was a great story, so some people pretended it was true, because they couldn't comprehend genuine politics.

Ignoring this, he pointed out a photograph of a Gemini 10 astronaut, in a water tank, suited up, simulating weightlessness months before the launch. Next to this, a picture of him in space, floating in front of a star background.

It's the same picture, with stars superimposed. He said it as a challenge, making me wish I'd saved my profanity.

I assured him it was coincidence, and he chuckled, because he knew how I valued the word.

There were more photographs, statistics, a picture of a book called *Man Never Went to the Moon*, which he said had been banned. The truth is that nobody published it because it was crap.

Special effects, he said, closing the magazine.

When I was about to speak, he asked why it bothered me.

This stuff bothers me because it is a lie, which people think can be made true, if it's repeated often enough. In space, astronauts are said to be disappointed by the stars, because they don't look any brighter. Being sensitive to the red end of the spectrum means that losing the atmosphere doesn't improve the spectacle. At many times, in low orbit, the stars are wiped out by the halo of the earth. It's easier to see the heavens lying on your back in England. And yet how many times have I heard people say that the stars are five times brighter in space.

As I explained this, Patrick fixed his attention behind me, but I refused to let him distract me, and finished what I was saying.

Fair enough, he said, if that's what you think.

*

Most people, if you ask them, have never watched the stars come out. I must ask about this with a tone of accusation, because I always hear excuses. It's too cold, my eyes aren't good enough, the sky's polluted around here, it's always cloudy. They think you need an observatory, a high place, miles from any town. On a clear night, all you need is space.

I picked Katie up at the end of her road, pleased to see her in jeans and an untucked French Connection T-shirt. If she had bothered to dress up, wasting time on makeup and hair spray, I'd have had a more difficult task, directing her attention from potential contact, to the opening of her senses.

She didn't question the fact that I drove over the bridge to Walney, didn't ask where we were going. I said I hoped she wouldn't be cold, as we turned on to the clubhouse track. At one point you have to cross a taxiway, and I remembered to halt, checking left and right before driving forward. It was normal for me to walk here, and I couldn't remember the last time I'd driven.

Half a moon was visible, but the stars were a few minutes away, and Katie was looking at the coast, where the lights at the

Lucas garage were already on. Pointing at the clubhouse, she said she could see it from where she worked, but always thought it was larger.

Motioning for her to follow, I walked behind the clubhouse, past the clicking anemometers, into a grassed area beside runway 35. The ground was dry, so we sat there and watched the sky break into light.

In films, whenever there is a poignant meeting under the stars, they cut to a long shot of the firmament, and I cringe, hoping there won't be a shooting star. There always is. Some hand-drawn sparkler, crawling across at the wrong angle. It doesn't matter how much they spend on the rest of the special effects, they always mess this one up. Shooting stars are beautiful, but they aren't nearly so bright as depicted. They move faster than in the films, so quick you see them more as a memory than an observation.

Katie was polite enough to listen as I explained. It must have been dawning on her by now that this wasn't an ordinary meeting, that I wouldn't be putting my arm around her. It was too soon to explain that any attraction she felt was an accident of the process, so instead, I showed her some constellations, and she tried to learn them.

The W of Cassiopeia led us to the Milky Way, and I tried to give her an idea of the distances and numbers involved. I explained that we were looking back in time, that the nearest star was so far away, its light reached us years late. The further away we looked, the further back in time we could see. I got the impression she thought I was explaining something hidden, as though we were the only ones who saw stars this way. To ground her again, I said that we never really see the surface of a star, the way we can with a planet; we only see a collection of its diffractive light.

Is this all a part of it? she asked.

You know what's happening then?

She said she had an idea. I tried not to look too surprised at her perception, and told her that I was only helping her with observation. It wasn't a requirement that she learn every constellation and statistic about the sky.

I must have been quiet, thinking about this – wondering whether I was boring her, trying to work out how she knew what was happening – because she disturbed me by telling me to carry on.

Holding my hand at arms length, I showed her how to calculate degrees of arc in the sky. From Segin to Caph is twenty degrees; the same as spread fingers. A fist is equal to nine degrees, taking you to Schedir. A thumb width marks two degrees back up to Achird.

I told her that you can blot out the moon with your little finger, because that digit is worth a full degree, the moon only half. Instead of trying this she held her palm against the sky, eyes focusing through it. The flesh in her hand was the colour of an X-ray, her fingers acting like a lens, moonlight bleaching on to her face. She pulled her palm aside, refusing to look at me, letting her head move backwards so she could see nothing other than the sky.

She asked me if I was going to show her inside the clubhouse, then said, Because I know you're not going to kiss me.

It must have been said to make me feel guilty, and to spoil my judgement. It was easier to take her inside than to hold her. She made a point of looking directly at me, while I struggled with her comment.

The door to the clubhouse was unlocked, and I went in first, telling her we wouldn't put on the lights. Pushing the table aside I started to bring on the silence, and Katie must have noticed, because she stayed close to the door, folding her arms as though frozen. The vibration of the anemometer was gone, our feet on the floorboards sounding far away. With a space cleared, I looked at Katie, willing her to come into the middle of the room.

When she was in the centre, I sat on the lone chair and completed the silence. I could have explained the process to her prior to this, but anything I might come up with would be too personal. Being the victim would be confusing, but it was the best way to initiate her. The rest of us weren't due for a meeting, having been through the rage a week earlier, so she would be let off lightly, with a minimal amount of corruption to digest. This confidence was destroyed when I brought the threads forward, and felt the size of the broken structure I'd picked up in The Lamb. It resisted, bloating in my stomach and lungs. Katie drew up a chair, but I was too distracted by the scrape of pain to realise what she was doing. When she put her hands together on her lap, and widened her eyes into a black stare, I tried to speak. My larynx vibrated, but the silence took the words, and I found myself kneeling on the floor.

Unprepared, I bit my tongue, the vast breaths I made forcing blood to drizzle between my teeth as the rage enveloped me. My bones thickened, muscle banding around them, my stomach gurgling and burning, heart smacking panic.

It's easy to describe the rage as all-consuming, because it is so violent you feel that you will break your bones or scream yourself mad. Despite this, a part of your mind remains unaffected. It's the same part of you that talks for long time, slowly and in detail, while you're crashing your car. The same part that observes rationally, knowing what a fool you look, when you're arguing. Psychologists believe that when the mind begins to work faster, this produces the illusion of slower time; during an emergency, time is suppressed by the speed of existence. The voice though, this calm observer, is a mystery. It could be primitive fragment of personality, or the true self sought by mystic traditions.

Mine was concerned, hoping that Katie Oswald knew how to dissipate the energy once it had been pushed inside me. If not, I could try to release it myself, spew it back at her, but seeing how competent she was with the power, I knew that wouldn't be a good idea.

There is usually a point at which the anger peaks, when everything has been taken into the victim. This is when the others are free to take the residue and use it. My view of Katie was unclear, watered by tears, darkened through lack of oxygen, but she was making signs with her hands, trying to get hold of something. A victim is supposed to remain free of contamination, to allow a pure influx, which could be why her flowing gestures were having no effect. The ritual failed, and I remained swollen with the surplus, which combined with my unreleased threads. Carried by the momentum of my fury, I couldn't resist opening them up.

When you see slow motion film of a drop of water splashing into a pond, there is a moment when the surface becomes spiked, like a crown, each pin of liquid releasing another drop of water. When the distortion erupted from me, it looked like that for a second, then inflated, each tendril warping.

There was a smell of petrol, and something sweaty, like onions and hair.

The feeling was similar to the few seconds of dizziness that occur when you're about to faint or be sick, except that it went on and on. My vision diminished, so that it was like looking through brown paper. My body must have slumped because my face was pushed against the floorboards, tongue touching the wood, skin sinking into the cracks. All that I could do was watch my breathing, making sure it continued, trying to ignore the fever wetting my clothes.

As the shivering relaxed, it was obvious that several hours had passed, because dawn was underway. The sky was busy with seagulls, their call closer than usual, as they used low air currents to soar over the grass at speed. I hadn't been asleep, but the shock must have disrupted my perception. The door remained open, but there was no sign of Katie, and I thought she must have left as soon as her efforts went astray.

Standing up, I could tell there was no physical damage, but felt weak, as though I had flu. I could use the phone, to contact Donald, get Patrick over, but I felt guilty for having caused this, especially in our retreat. It was also likely that, along with myself, nobody would know how to deal with the distortion, or what we should do about Katie Oswald.

*

The first indication that defences were in place came when I walked past The Lamb. My mind didn't blank out, as you might expect, but I was hungry, anxious to get home and feast my way through the cupboards. Most of all I wanted to be alone in bed, asleep. In itself, that should have caught my attention first thing in the morning, but it was only when I turned into the town hall square, that I remembered why I was out at all.

It was impressive in one way, that she could set up protection so effectively, but also naive. Although I might be distracted for a while, maybe even hours if she protected the pub correctly, it wouldn't keep me away for long. As it was, her workings confirmed there was something to hide. It would be foolhardy to rush in, because if she was capable of spreading her effects around in this way, her secondary defences could be more powerful.

Distraction techniques work on your weaknesses. She couldn't set up a barrier that would numb my mind, or prevent me from thinking about her. What she could do was weaken me, make alternative desires more consuming. It's like catching a cold. You're always riddled with influenza germs, but you need to believe in a cold before it will bring you down. If you become cold, wet, or weakened through upset, you give in to it, accept the cold, and it becomes a part of your life. It's the idea that's infectious. The barrier was meant to work in the same way, bringing on hunger, fatigue, making me want to do anything other than chase after her.

The door was locked, and it was obvious after a couple of minutes knocking, that Ian and his parents had been persuaded to keep me out. I went into the car park at the back, testing both doors, the toilet and kitchen windows, and accepted that I would have to break in. It's not something I'm trained in, but it would be too much trouble to seek out an accomplice. After another attempt at knocking, I dragged an aluminium barrel from between the Coke crates, debating whether to lob it at the kitchen window, or use it to climb to a higher level. Losing patience, still troubled by the weak hunger, I opted for the former. The barrel was heavier than it looked, once hoisted to chest height, but that meant it passed through the glass easily.

It took me a minute or two to arrange crates beneath the ledge, and climb through without being sliced. I began to wonder whether anyone was in, because no matter what Katie had been up to, the noise should have attracted attention.

The internal doors were unlocked, and I was working out which would be the best way to get to Ian's room, when I found him in the hall. He was naked, apart from a towel, the same sallow colour as his body. One hand gripped a bulge where the material joined up, the other was held palm out at me. At first I thought he was urging me to leave or be quiet, because he kept looking at the stairs where his parents would be, but his face had the sorry expression of somebody who is about to be slapped. He was trying to calm me down.

I asked him if she was here, but he looked so confused, I thought something had been done to keep him quiet. His beard was wet, clogging in curls, and he licked at the edge of them.

Is she here? I repeated, and he said something that sounded like, I'll get what I deserve.

When I asked about his parents, expecting them to slow my

progress, he said they weren't present, he was alone, but refused to say why.

Unwilling to wait for him to make sense, I went into the public bar, then the lounge, checking for damage. There was none, which either meant the pub had been closed for the past few days, or somebody was stealing from me.

Ian was in the same place when I came back. Asking him who had been allowed to take the pain, I could see he was trying to think of some way he could mislead me, but the situation had stunned him.

I asked him again if she had been here.

He said it hadn't worked yet, so I left him and went upstairs. The hallway was built on several levels, each room at a different height. All the doors were ajar, except one, which made my search easier.

If it wasn't for my background, I could have missed the devices in Ian's bedroom, because they were simple. His room was small, meaning that the few ornaments he kept were clustered together on the window-sill. The water jar, with an onion growing in it, could have escaped my attention, except that I saw a distortion shaping the air around it. Its roots were as white as rice, new shoots breaking through the ginger shell. Around the base of the jar were five stones, ordinary enough to have been taken from any beach, apart from the circles and lines that were scratched on to them. Around these, traces of salt.

Ian stood in the doorway, and it was tempting to smash his jar against the wall, or throw it at him, but instead I let him watch as I put my hand into its puny energy and charmed it away. The onion couldn't look any different to him, but he knew what I had done.

Sitting on the bed, I invited him to come next me. I don't know why he thought I could be violent, but he was afraid. It was possible that he'd been told I could hurt him in other ways. Over the years, his awareness of my search for pain may have been off-putting, making me appear more sinister than I am. He sat beside me, looking at his knees, his beard and hair congealing as they dried.

I asked him what she promised him, what the deal had been, and he rubbed his face, his hand coming away wet. He said he didn't know who I meant.

Katie Oswald?

She was for Patrick, he said.

It wouldn't matter if I looked shocked and showed the holes in my knowledge, because if it came down to it, I could frighten any information I wanted out of Ian. I tried to stay clam, not for the sake of secrecy, but because his words were a surprise.

Patrick set this up? I asked, pointing at his crude alter.

He said yes, his tongue sticking. They agreed to work together a month ago, he explained. When Ian granted access to the pub, after closing time, Patrick offered to share some of the produce. A trace of the energy would be put into Ian's efforts; he looked at the onion. It was laughable to think that such a physically oriented ritual would have any effect, but more disturbing was that Patrick had encouraged him.

Ian didn't know what Patrick was doing at night, but it was noisy and lasted for hours. He thought it was something more advanced than usual, not just taking the pain, but regurgitating it. Then he muttered something about his parents never hearing. They've been kept out of the way, he said.

Was Katie ever with him? I asked.

He'd never met her, and from what he could gather, Patrick hadn't been able to get near to her as quickly as intended.

At this point, I tried to slow him down, and asked him to get dressed, to make him less nervous. He turned away, perhaps thinking that the sight of his arse was less offensive than a full frontal.

When dressed, he explain everything as he knew it, pausing over aspects that he didn't understand, trying to make his betrayal of me sound less deliberate, suggesting coercion, repeating aspects of his weakness. His story was confused by mistaken beliefs about our system, and from what I could tell, Patrick had exaggerated our abilities.

There was never any promise that Ian would be initiated into the circle, but he would be allowed to perform his own ritual. That was why he'd turned against me; Patrick offered him something in return, when all I did was tell him to keep quiet.

I asked him what it was for, what he hoped to gain. He was using it as an enchantment, to attract somebody. His lips folded together, wobbling as he explained; he said a girl's name, nobody I knew. Then he told me it was the same for Patrick. He was trying to bring Katie into the fold, but it was getting out of hand. Something had gone wrong.

Two hours earlier, Patrick had woken Ian up, demanding access to the building, then moved from room to room, furious, chanting something unintelligible. Ian couldn't get much sense out of him, and tried instead to keep out of his way, until his procedure was closed. He confirmed that Patrick was alone; there was no sign of Katie. From the few things he picked up, it sounded as though Katie had vanished.

I told him to think carefully, to remember whether anything had ever been said, about where Patrick might go in an emergency. Nothing came to mind. Fear might have kept Ian's mouth shut, if Patrick threatened him but I'm convinced he didn't know where either of them were.

Can't you see them? he asked, presuming I could close my eyes and find the answers.

I told him it doesn't work like that, and left him to guess at what I meant. Although I could find anything I wanted, or see a scene in detail, such perceptions have to be performed as a closing to the rage. Patrick may have found a way around this, but I didn't know any way to use the skills without a gathering. To solve a problem like this, I might need more than my fair share of the residue, and I wasn't even sure whether a meeting would be possible. If we worked now, how would we cope with the force at the clubhouse? Besides which, the rage wasn't due for some time, and if Patrick was this determined to pervert the process, I didn't have much time.

Ian asked me whether I would still be dropping in, and I said that I would, but not in the evenings. Once this was cleared up, I would continue to gather as required, but he was no longer my friend. I reminded him that I was the one doing a favour, and that he should be grateful.

When I stood up to leave, he cried, fingers wiping at his tears, his mouth and nose glossy with mucus, running into his beard. It was tempting to stay and watch, because from the back of his neck, a fine line of pain trickled up, making it look as though he was about to be hung. Before it was fully established, I closed the door, because I have no doubt he was crying about the girl he couldn't capture, rather than the loss of his friend.

*

There were other places to fill up, but I let the Lucas garage be the augury for my direction. I was served by the owner's brother, Fernleigh. He was a favourite with the kids around here, who would cycle out of town to buy sweets from him, because he had no voice box. Some cancer or other had caused it to be removed, and a whirring prosthetic was jammed into this throat, which people said made him sound like a Dalek. That was a crude description, because the sound was more like somebody purring through a fan. A string-knit scarf was folded around his neck. His head was bald, fat and brown. I asked him to put in five-ninety five, as it was all the change I had, and I didn't want to break into a tenner.

When the pump was in the cradle, I asked Fernleigh about Katie Oswald, and he hummed, his mouth shaping the words. Fhiffe-nhine-fhiffe. He was asking me for payment.

Do you know what's happened to her? I asked. Shouldn't she be here?

Holding one hand out, he drew a line down his palm. It could have been a sign, but he repeated the phrase. Fhiffe-nhine-fhiffe. Asking after Patrick was a waste of time, met with the same demand.

I told him I was heading north, and he held up one finger, nodding, a sign of agreement, then held out his hand.

Fernleigh's attitude was a relief in one way, and I smiled as I pulled out, thinking how frustrating it would be if he did know what was going on. I could picture him explaining it all, revealing where Patrick and Katie were, and all I'd hear was a spinning thrum of air, ornamented with consonants.

My car is less than efficient, so it could have run out anywhere from Sellafield onward. The needle settled beneath the red line on the bypass around Workington, but it was after Maryport that the engine faltered.

A sign said Parking 1 Mile, but I pulled up on the stony beach, the waves closer than felt safe. Before I switched off the engine, it paused, caught for a second, and stopped. Across Allonby bay, the mountains of Dumfriesshire, were so insubstantial they could be mistaken for cloud. The sea stank of shit and vinegar, the water distributing straw, broken wood and plastic between the rocks.

I was probably meant to make it as far as the car park, but

chose to walk from this settling point. The first path I found went past the edge of a golf course, up short, steep hill. When it levelled out, the countryside was familiar; flat fields, with occasional fences, and in the whole expanse, perhaps ten trees.

It took me half an hour to find a sign of activity. There was a building ahead of me, a short distance from the footpath, no larger than one room. Made from old stone and sloping tiles, it was windowless, and I could see no door. There didn't appear to be any path, either from this side or the other. When I stopped, there was a sound like a hissing cistern, something clicking inside.

Looking up and down the path, I couldn't see any other building, any reason for it to be there. The door must be around the other side. I could climb over the barbed wire fence, see if the door was open or locked. If it was open, there would be no harm in having a look inside.

I listened for the sound again, but it was difficult to tell whether there was anything. The only movement came from two cabbage white moths, which spiralled around each other in front of me, the light on them leaving trails of afterimage. I blinked, checked up and down the path. There was no one there. It would take less than a minute to get over, have a look and get back.

Once over the fence, I saw that the grass around the building was more succulent than any I had seen for weeks. Kneeling to run my fingers through it, it felt like hair, rather than the dry, bristly grass I was used to. It was so thick, my feet left imprints in it, the blades all combed in the direction of my progress.

The door was around the back, unlocked, half open, its wood warm to the touch. The brightness outside made it too dark to see in, and I knew it would take a moment for my eyes to adjust. Stepping inside, the air cooled. Seams of light came in where the slates were loose against stones. The first shape I saw was a sink, its outside edge darkened by dust-filled cracks. Inside the bowl was clean, because a brass tap was running water into it. There was no splutter, only the even seethe of water releasing into the plug hole.

I touched the tap, putting my hands into the water, wondering how long it had been left on. I turned the tap off, and it stopped without dripping. As the bowl emptied, the plug hole made a sighing as it swallowed the last drops.

Looking further in, I saw that the floor was made of compact dirt. Kneeling, like somebody about to be sick, with his back to me, Patrick circled his hands over the soil, but there was no noise. If he was speaking any invocation it went unheard. I reached for his shoulder, but before my hand was near him, the image spread, then vanished. Whatever he'd been working on was complete. There was a rough circle of wax stains, each charred with the remains of wick, but he'd taken the residue with him.

*

Nothing comes as a shock. Whatever happens, no matter how unusual or upsetting, part of you thinks, I knew it. You hear people say this all the time, after accidents that came from nowhere, or when a faithful partner is caught with her pants down. I knew this would happen. It's nothing to do with sub-conscious doubts, or body language cues; in the most basic terms, its precognition.

If you pay attention to these feelings, and work with them, you can tell when something is going to happen. They're no use to you in hindsight, so you must learn to catch them before the event.

It was throwing out time as I drove back into Barrow, the pubs putting people on the street, where they continued to drink from smuggled bottles, too skint for the clubs, reluctant to go home. Having spent more hours than I wanted to walking into Maryport for fuel, I was tired and frustrated. Driving between pizza boxes and smashed glass was difficult enough, but it was made treacherous by men in white shirts leaping in front of the car with their arms out, trying to frighten me. I was tempted to step on the throttle, instead of the brake, but smiled until they moved out of the way. In return they patted the side of the car as I went past, making whooping noises. Following that, I was a bit reluctant to park up in the centre, so drove further out. This gave me the chance to drive down Patrick's road. As expected his curtains were open, the lights out. I used his parking space, locked the car, and went back into town.

For the first time since spring I was able to see my own breath. It was cold and cloudless, but the stars were hidden by the haze of streetlight. I'm not a nervous person, but I don't walk round with my hands in my pockets at that time of night.

The square was well lit, so it was easy to see the state of the place, but I was struck more by the smell of beer and sick, and the noise. Talking at pub volume, the voices mingled over each other so there were no recognisable words; it sounded like a moan, punctuated by shouts. You'd think with all that drinking going on there would be laughter, but even when I listened out for it, there was none.

Standing by the police vans, so that I felt safer, I took my time to have a good look around. There were lots of people I could have followed, if they were alone, but most moved on in groups, or climbed into taxis. I needed a loner, which meant it would have to be a man. Even if I found a suitable women, following her would get me into trouble. When the crowd was getting thin, I accepted that I was in the wrong place, and crossed the square. It would be easier to find somebody alone if I could get to a quieter area.

Somebody was singing a couple of streets away, each line ending with a wail, which became more angry, until there was no song, only shouting. I ran to the top of the street, so I could pass the end of other roads, trying locate him again, but the wind blew straight in my ear, making it difficult to hear.

I was trying too hard. You can't force these situations, by chasing people down. If you stand quietly, away from view, the right person will cross your path. Ideally you want somebody who is lost, but just about past caring. The cold keeps this type moving, which is better. If they once slump, you can't get anything out of them.

The man I chose was older than usual, being well in his forties, but thin. All his clothes were blue denim, shirt, jacket, jeans. He walked in bursts, pausing to steady himself, before setting off again. Afraid of bumping into lampposts, he held his hands out as he passed them. He didn't see me, so I stepped after him walking as quietly as I could. I chose him because, rather than singing or shouting, he was muttering. I couldn't help but think he was whispering secrets.

When I was close enough to hear him – the first audible words being something about a broken window – he stopped and turned to face me.

Problem?

To hear him speak so clearly, when he'd been muttering was

unexpected. I stopped walking, when he turned, which made it obvious I was following him. If I'd carried on, I could have circled him, telling him to calm down, making out nothing was amiss.

What's going on? he said.

Nothing mate, I said, trying to look in the same state as he was, pretending to hold myself up against the air. It didn't convince him, and as I tried to get past he moved to the side to stop me.

No fucking way, he said.

It wouldn't take much to knock him down. Being so drunk, he would be slow, and I wouldn't need to do anything other than fling him over. So long as he wasn't carrying a knife, I'd get out of this all right. I was annoyed at myself for wasting an opportunity, so in an attempt to recover the situation, I told him to go home.

You should of listened, he said. I thought this was another threat, but saw that he was looking at the pavement, not at me. If he was talking to himself again, that was a good sign.

Should of listened.

Listened to what?

You should of. Listened to her. When she said.

That was all I could make out, because his mouth was so full of spit, he was unable to speak any more. If he once puked, there'd be no use for him, and the way he leaned over, hands on his thighs, I thought it was going to end there. He was panting to make himself recover.

I want to go home, he said, looking at me as though I was his friend. It almost felt like we'd been in town together, and were helping each other to struggle home. He said it again, so I asked him where he lived.

Take me home. You should've taken me home.

Where do you live?

He pointed, so I put my arm on his back, and helped him to walk. It was the opposite direction to the one he'd been going when I found him. Nothing else came from him for a while, because he was concentrating on pointing. We went back through the town square, glass crunching underfoot. It was colder, the pavement slabs textured with frost, except where people had urinated against the walls, their piss sticking in patches that refused to freeze.

The clubs would be coming out soon, so I urged my companion to hurry it up, trying to get him to stand straighter. The way he held on to me, I wondered if he knew who I was; he was clinging like he was my brother.

Do you know where you are?

His voice was clear again, the way it had been when he threatened me

Do you live around here?

He went down, his hands melting the frost. He spread his jaw, a watery line of mucus leading the way for gobs of greasy vomit. It went over his hands, but he wasn't moving any more. The only sign that he was conscious, apart from his posture, was the way he spat between convulsions, getting rid of the wet crumbs clogging his mouth.

If he hadn't asked me that question, I would have left it at that, walked back to my car or straight home. Even though I was standing at the end of Katie's road, in the place where I'd picked her up the night before, it hadn't struck me as significant. Only as I thought about his question, and looked at the street names, did it dawn on me. This should have been the first place I looked.

I thought back to the morning, retracing my route from Walney. From the bridge, I'd come here, intending to go to her house. If she wasn't there, I was going to quiz her parents and track her down, but I passed the end of the street, going to The Lamb instead. Once I detected the barriers there, and discovered them to be Patrick's, that prevented me from thinking further back. Unwittingly, his bungled efforts made hers a better secret. I was astonished that I could have missed something so obvious, for so many hours. Whatever else she'd achieved, her distraction was successful. All day, when I thought about Katie's location, I never once pictured her house; I just kept presuming she'd done a runner, disappearing like Patrick, and yet there was no evidence to make me think that. It was quite possible she was at home now, with her parents.

The man in denim got up and I backed away, because I didn't want him to hold me now that he was covered in sick. He was no use any more, so I nodded an acknowledgement, smiled. He followed me, holding his hands out as though they'd been burnt, but walked slowly enough for me to get away from him.

There were no lights on in Katie's house. Before I let anything distract me, I knocked on the door. Still no lights, not even in the neighbouring houses, even though that usually seems to happen when you knock for people late at night.

As the man in denim approached, I hoped he was her father or brother, that he could let me in, but he went past without a word. Staring at the front door, I thought over my options. If her parents were in, I could make enough noise to wake them, but I didn't want too much attention. Having got this close, I didn't want to leave, in case I managed to forget again. It was unlikely, because once you know the reality of a situation, it's difficult to be deceived.

The nearest phone box was round the corner. Directories gave me her number, and I let it ring, wishing I could see the house, for lights coming on. When it was answered, the person on the other end said, Is that you? She didn't sound tired, but her voice was nervous.

It's me, I said.

Patrick? she asked.

No Katie, it's me.

There was no sound, until she asked where I was. When I told her she said, You'd better come round then.

*

Change is accumulative. It's the stream of existence that makes us who we are. Life-changing moments are only made meaningful by their context within the ordinary. The way Katie spoke to me that night couldn't have changed me in itself; I wouldn't have been moved, if it wasn't for the things we already shared. This probably sounds obvious, but it's surprising how often you forget it.

It was unfair of me to say she was misled by the changes, or by Patrick's interference. The truth, she explained, was that she wanted to be with me, because she saw the way I watched her.

You can't be a victim of somebody else's feelings, I said.

She shook her head, assuring me that wasn't what she meant, but then said, If you didn't feel something for me, this wouldn't have happened.

In a way, I think she was right. I thought Patrick was a fool, for sulking around her, hiding his feelings, trying to use his skills to attract her, when he could have just talked, but Katie made me realise that I'd done the same thing. The difference was, I didn't even have the guts to admit it.

By morning we had forgotten to whisper, and when she heard her Dad go to the toilet, she suggested I leave. I don't know whether it was the exhaustion getting to me, or the cold dawn wind, but when she closed the door, my eyes were watering.

*

We haven't seen Patrick since, but I think about him every day. I miss working the airfield with him, and walking back when it was too late to fly. Only now it's over, do I know why we never took our cars; we wanted a reason to walk home together, watching the sun go down.

He used to remind me that sunsets are caused by pollution and dirt, the sun's rays red-shifted by the stuff we choke on. Sometimes I'd counter this with romantic notions, telling him that pollen and bonfire smoke stained our light. Or I'd challenge his cynicism with facts, saying the hue was caused by the depth of atmosphere, the angle of rays. It was one of those ongoing disputes, which we never cared to resolve.

We walked to the south end of Walney, on a path through the seagull sanctuary, between the down and fluff of nesting birds. The gulls in the air switched from shadows to flecks of red as they turned. I could smell broken eggs and the rotten bodies of the dead, laid out amongst the living. Some were fresh and intact, others hollowed by decay, the oldest nothing more than yellow wet bones.

Looking north, I saw the glider coming in to land, wondering out loud who was up there so late. Even from this distance, I thought I could hear the whining of its wings.

Patrick was going on about the mess in the air, saying it was chemicals and filth, but he couldn't take his eyes off the sun. Where it touched the sea, the scarlet edge was pulled on to the water, like surface tension.

When we reached the bridge, I spotted the moon, magnified and coloured like soup, rising over the slag heap behind Barrow.

I prefer to watch the moon when it appears on a winter morning, its shadows as blue as the sky it rests in. Something from childhood means I can never let go of the idea that the moon comes out at night. When I see the full sphere of it in day-time, it feels like a reward.

I still own a telescope, but it's years since I've used it. With a strong enough lens the planets took on form. Easiest of all was Venus, a baby crescent, brighter than stars. Jupiter was the colour of a tooth, with Io, Ganymede, Calisto and Europa a line of points around it. When focused correctly, it made the stars sharper, smaller, more difficult to appreciate. The moon was brought close, but it moved away as I watched. By the time I'd lined up on it, the edge was sliding out of sight. This disturbed me, because it wasn't the movement of the moon I could see, but the spin of the earth. I don't like to be reminded how fast the days are passing.

Outstanding Paperback Originals from The Do-Not Press:

It's Not A Runner Bean
by Mark Steel

"If only all subversives could be like him" — *NME*

The life of a Slightly Successful Comedian can include a night spent on bare floorboards next to a pyromaniac squatter in Newcastle, followed by a day in Chichester with someone so aristocratic, they speak without ever moving their lips.

From his standpoint behind the microphone, Mark Steel (of Radio 4's *The Mark Steel Solution*) is in the perfect position to view all human existence. Which is why this book – like his act and his broadcasts – is opinionated, passionate, and extremely funny.

"I wish I'd had this to read when I was shagging him..." — Jo Brand

ISBN 1 899344 12 8 — £5.99

The Users
by Brian Case

The welcome return of Brian Case's brilliantly original '60s cult classic.

"A remarkable debut" —Anthony Burgess

"Why Case's spiky first novel from 1968 should have languished for nearly thirty years without a reprint must be one of the enigmas of modern publishing. Mercilessly funny and swaggeringly self-conscious, it could almost be a template for an early Martin Amis."
— *Sunday Times*

ISBN 1 899344 05 5— £5.99

Life In The World Of Women
a collection of vile, dangerous and loving stories **by Maxim Jakubowski**

Maxim Jakubowski's dangerous and erotic stories of war between the sexes are collected here for the first time, including three major new pieces. Taking in aspects of crime noir, erotica, romance and gritty social drama, *Life In The World Of Women* confirms Maxim Jakubowski as one of Britain's finest and hardest-hitting writers.

"Whatever else it might be – romantic pornography or pornographic romance – *Life* is a bold experiment in self-mythologising fiction."
— Nicholas Royle, *Time Out*

"Demonstrates that erotic fiction can be amusing, touching, spooky and even (at least occasionally) elegant. Erotic fiction seems to be Jakubowski's true metier. These stories have the hard sexy edge of Henry Miller and the redeeming grief of Jack Kerouac. A first class collection." — Ed Gorman, *Mystery Scene* (USA)

ISBN 1 899344 06 3 — £6.99

BLOODLINES the cutting-edge crime and mystery imprint...

Smalltime
by Jerry Raine
Smalltime is a taut, psychological crime thriller, set among the seedy world of petty criminals and no-hopers. In this remarkable début, Jerry Raine shows just how easily curiosity can turn into fear amid the horrors, despair and despondency of life lived a little too near the edge.

"Jerry Raine's *Smalltime* carries the authentic whiff of sleazy nineties Britain. He vividly captures the world of stunted ambitions and their evil consequences."— Simon Brett

ISBN 1 899344 13 6 — £5.99

Perhaps She'll Die!
by John B Spencer
Giles could never say 'no' to a woman... any woman. But when he tangled with Celeste, he made a mistake... A bad mistake.

Celeste was married to Harry, and Harry walked a dark side of the street that Giles – with his comfortable lifestyle and fashionable media job – could only imagine in his worst nightmares. And when Harry got involved in nightmares, people had a habit of getting hurt.

Set against the boom and gloom of eighties Britain, *Perhaps She'll Die!* is classic *noir* with a centre as hard as toughened diamond.

ISBN 1 899344 14 4 — £5.99

Fresh Blood
edited by Mike Ripley & Maxim Jakubowski
"Move over Agatha Christie and tell Sherlock the News!" This landmark anthology features the cream of the British New Wave of crime writers: John Harvey, Mark Timlin, Chaz Brenchley, Russell James, Stella Duffy, Ian Rankin, Nicholas Blincoe, Joe Canzius, Denise Danks, John B Spencer, Graeme Gordon, the two editors, and a previously unpublished extract from the late Derek Raymond. Includes an introduction from each author explaining their views on crime fiction in the '90s and a comprehensive foreword on the genre from Angel-creator, Mike Ripley.

ISBN 1 899344 03 9 — £6.99

Quake City
by John B Spencer
The third novel to feature Charley Case, the hard-boiled investigator of the future. But of a future that follows the 'Big One of Ninety-Seven' – the quake that literally rips California apart and makes LA an Island.

"Classic Chandleresque private eye tale, jazzed up by being set in the future... but some things never change – PI Charley Case still has trouble with women and a trusty bottle of bourbon is always at hand. An entertaining addition to the private eye canon."
— John Williams, *Mail on Sunday*

ISBN 1 899344 02 0 — £5.99

The Do-Not Press
Fiercely Independent Publishing

Keep in touch with what's happening at the cutting edge of independent British publishing.

Join The Do-Not Press Information Service and receive advance information of all our new titles, as well as news of events and launches in your area, and the occasional free gift and special offer.

Simply send your name and address to:
The Do-Not Press (Dept. WYHM)
PO Box 4215
London
SE23 2QD

There is no obligation to purchase and
no salesman will call.